遥かなる旅路

キーツ・エッセイ・漢詩

高橋 雄四郎 著

音羽書房鶴見書店

まえがき

　60余年前、大分市上戸次大字利光の片田舎から笈を負うて上京。紆余曲折をへて英国風景画論を加え、キーツ研究3部作を終えた。いま宮沢賢治の自然観を模索する段階である。

　挫折、失意、再起の現実。だが成長を秘めた魂の牧歌（自然）性に潜む妖精を歌うキーツの想像力——Negative Capability——の永遠性。それはシェイクスピアと重なり、風景画 (J. Constable) のイメージと共振する。筆者の精神史における郷里（牧歌）——自己との戦い（叙事詩）とも響き合う。

　過去は時空を経、追憶・夢となり神話化（ギ・ロ神話にあらず）し、未来は現在となる。第一部「神話と現実——キーツ詩におけるアポロ」、第二部・エッセイ "Memories and Ideas"、第三部「漢詩のほそみち——春夏秋冬」。何れも美真に近づこうとする筆者の魂の軌跡を反映させる。

　70歳を過ぎ、英文エッセイ、漢詩に興味を抱きはじめた。大切なのは起承転結。語ろうとするテーマを中心に、文章の簡潔な展開を心がけなければならない。両者軌を一にする。読後の余韻も欲しい。漢詩の源泉は、戦時中も三年次まで必修の母校旧制大分中学にある。気がつくと名詩暗誦の習慣が身についていた。春の宵、緑の木陰、秋の夕暮、冬の夜など折に触れいま情感に浸る。孤独は先人との対話のひととき。今回は七言絶句のみ。マラルメのいう "pour moi, pour moi" にほかならない。

2017年7月吉日

　　　　　　　　　　　　　高橋　雄四郎

感謝をこめて　この書を　妻恭子と
遥かなる郷里の祖霊に捧げる

遥かなる旅路

キーツ・エッセイ・漢詩

目　次

まえがき ・・・ i

第 1 部
神話と現実——キーツ詩におけるアポロ ・・・・・・・・・・ 1

第 2 部
Memories and Ideas ・・・・・・・・・・・・・・・・・・・・・・・・ 41

I Past and Present

My Biographical Sketch ・・・・・・・・・・・・・・・・・・・・・ 44
My Beloved Teacher Homma Hisao ・・・・・・・・・・・・・ 46
A Photograph ・・・・・・・・・・・・・・・・・・・・・・・・・・・・・ 48
Newly built Gravestone ・・・・・・・・・・・・・・・・・・・・・ 50
A Fairyland ・・・・・・・・・・・・・・・・・・・・・・・・・・・・・・ 52
Fairyland Again ・・・・・・・・・・・・・・・・・・・・・・・・・・・ 54
An Optimistic Driver ・・・・・・・・・・・・・・・・・・・・・・・ 56
To Bury the Hair and Nail in our Ancestral Graveyard
・・ 58
Nine Minutes ・・・・・・・・・・・・・・・・・・・・・・・・・・・・・ 60
A Couple of my Front Teeth ・・・・・・・・・・・・・・・・・・ 62
My Friend, Dr. Furukawa ・・・・・・・・・・・・・・・・・・・・ 64
Aging is an Unknown Journy ・・・・・・・・・・・・・・・・・ 66

II Seasons, Trees and Worms

The Rain in the Season for Leaf-buds to Grow ・・・・・・ 70
The Persimmon Tree in Early Spring ・・・・・・・・・・・・ 72
Little Creatures in the Soil ・・・・・・・・・・・・・・・・・・・ 74
A Whiff of Fresh Air ・・・・・・・・・・・・・・・・・・・・・・・・ 76

The *Kinmokusei* in our Garden 78
Fallen Leaves 80

III Wife and Husband

Communication between Kyoko and I 84
A Bottle of Sake and Youth 86
Our Vegetable Soup 88
Homemade Orange Marmalade Jam 90
March Cold in my Mind 92
June is near at Hand 94
Ireland, a Vision 96
Yoshiko, One Hundred and Three Years Old 98
Yoshiko, One Hundred and Four Years Old 100
Farewell to Yoshiko-san 102
Haircut 104
The Car for Ladies Only 106
Kyoko's Birthday 108

第3部

漢詩のほそみち──春・夏・秋・冬── 111

第一章　春 113

第二章　夏 140

第三章　秋 164

第四章　冬 182

あとがき 195

第1部
Part One

神話と現実
——キーツ詩におけるアポロ

(1)

　大地に生まれた魂は、何れ、天上に舞い戻る。生きていくプロセスで、人は悩み、焦り、苛立ち、立ち止まり、思索する。だが歳月とともに、死が視界に入りはじめ、天上を夢見ると安らぎを覚える。キーツ詩を俯瞰するとき、アポロの機能を備えたい、と彼は自らに言い聞かせていたのでないか。詩人の魂の軌跡はそのようにあとづけられる側面をもつ。医師を諦め、詩人の道を選んだ気迫が伝わってくる。対象に溶けこみ、カメレオンのように変化するキーツ。月（シンシア・ヘカテ・ダイアナ）との溶け合いと表裏する、予言者・医学・詩神を兼ねるアポロとの合体。成熟した理想の詩人への成長。原動力になるのは、自我 "Self" の消滅と、ネガティヴ・ケイパビリティ。以上の視点から、キーツ詩におけるアポロを見たい。

　最初にダフネ（月桂樹ローレル）・エピソードに触れよう。

　キューピッドは常に2種類の矢を用意している。先端に黄金のついた矢と、鉛のついた矢。後者の場合、この矢が当たると、異性に追いかけられるのが煩わしくなる。アポロは黄金の矢、ダフネは鉛の矢でそれぞれの胸を射抜かれる。アポロの前に姿を現したダフネは激しい恋心で夢中のアポロに追いかけられる。どんなに逃げても所詮、アポロの俊足にかなう筈はない。あわや腰に手が回わされかかったとき、彼女は父なる川の精に助けを求める。すると四肢は忽ち月桂樹に変わる。こうしてアポロの恋は、常緑エヴァグリーンの月桂樹＝月桂冠に象徴

第1部

されることになる。"evergreen" は永遠の青春、魂の不滅性を
表す。

アポロ頌歌

　　黄金いろめく西の宮殿広間の
　　自分の領地に　アポロよ　お前が落ち着くとき
　　英雄たちの功績　彼らの運命を熱烈に語り
　　歌いあげた　かつてのうたびとたちが
　　金剛石の竪琴（ライヤ）をしっかり抱え
　　光り輝く炎（ほのお）のようにたえまなく弦を煌めかせる。

　　ホメロス　その腕に想いをこめ　いくさを歌い語れば
　　竪琴の弦はぶわんぶわんと高鳴り
　　西の空もあたたかく輝いてくる
　　トランペットを遠くに響かせて。
　　だが何がこの強烈な驚きを創りだすのかと
　　彼の詩魂は　いのち甦る新鮮な眼差しで見守るのだ

　　そのとき　お前の広々とした神殿から　ゆたかな旋律が
　　聞こえてくる　竪琴（ライヤ）の弾き手はバージル
　　よろこびの魂がひとつひとつのコトバに宿り──
　　恍惚として宿るのだ　息もそぞろに。
　　その間　彼は歌う　弔い用の重ねられた薪の周りで

4

神話と現実——キーツ詩におけるアポロ

恐ろしい静寂がまた訪れる
待ちうけていた星ぼしがまたたく
月桂冠を巻いた貴人たちは息をひそめ
身じろぎひとつしない　荘重な旋律の果てるまで
ミルトンの雷風メロディの終わるまで身じろがない
やがて魅了された天空はもと通りの静寂となる

……………………………

だがアポロよ　お前が九人の詩神に加われば
歌う力はもっともっと強くなって
われらは地上でじっと耳かたむけるだろう
調べは消えずに余韻嫋々天空を満たし
美しい夕べの空を魅了する
みなうたびとの大いなる神・汝より天界の生を享けるのだ

（第8連）

沈む夕陽を歌う、いうなれば夕暮れの階調、「アポロ讃歌」。詩の中でキーツは、己が影響を受けた詩人たち（ホメロス、バージル、ミルトン、シェイクスピア、スペンサー、タッソー）を列挙する。彼らが死後、天上で、詩神アポロの前で、それぞれの作品を竪琴に合わせて披露している光景。黄金色に輝く竪琴が、アポロのイメージと重なる。詩は第8連に重点が置かれている。九人の詩神ミューズを従えるアポロに敵う者はいない。だがアポロの歌う詩、それは "evergreen"（月桂樹）——永遠の

第1部

青春、魂の不滅——を意味するだけであろうか？　ここでギリシャ神話におけるアポロを定義しておきたい。

　　　「天体の神として、アポロは、物理的調和の宇宙的システムを支配する。医療の神としては、人間の肉体的諸要素の調和を保つ。太陽神として彼は、時の経過、大地の果実の成熟を司る。詩歌の神として、人間の知性の成熟を支配し、調和のとれた表現という収穫において、人間の知性の結実をもたらす」[1]

さらに、予言者としての機能がある。外観は（黄金の弓／黄金の竪琴／黄金の髪の毛／黄金の炎もつ神／馬車駆けらせるもの）（「もう一つの‘アポロ頌歌’」1–5）として描かれている。

　詩人はアポロ神を独創的に歌う。キーツの究極の目標は、己の心にアポロを住みつかせ、自らがアポロ神になること。「驚異の年」"annus mirabilis"を前にして、姿を現す彼の「魂創造」寓話の骨子は、自らの体験を通し、他者の苦しみを己のものと感じうるようになるまで、魂を成長させることを意味している。人間の神への昇華。冒頭の「アポロ頌歌」は初期の作品であるが、その後、彼が辿る詩作の全プロセスを暗示している。この小論は、「頌歌」の基調をなす"golden color"を基軸に、一段また一段、高みに成長を遂げていく詩人の魂をギリシャ神話が、現実と溶け合う視点から跡づけるものである。

(2)

But when *Thou* joinest with the Nine,

And all the powers of song combine,

We listen here on earth:

The dying tones that fill the air,

And charm the ear of evening fair,

From thee, great God of Bards, receive their heavenly birth.

「アポロ頌歌」（第8連）

　さきに掲げた「アポロ頌歌」は、第8連に含意がある。前半3行が後半3行を支配している。アポロと9人の詩神たちは「地上の全ての調和の源泉」(the originators of all earthly harmony)[2]。このアロットの視点は、辺りを支配する "The dying tones" が夕暮れの色である点を強調。それは地上にも反映し、この黄金色は、第1連、6行目の "solid rays"（均質の、絶え間ない光）と呼応し、光と色によって奏でられる地上の音楽とイメージの点で重なる。「消えようとする天空を満たす調べ」は、沈みゆく夕暮れの大地の調べと呼応することになる。

The poetry of earth is ceasing never:

　On a lone winter evening, when the frost

　　Has wrought a silence, from the stove there shrills

The Cricket's song, in warmth increasing ever,

第 1 部

And seems to one in drowsiness half lost,

The Grasshopper's among some grassy hills.

December 30, 1816.

　　大地の詩は決して止むことはない
　　　孤独な冬の夕べにあっても　そのとき　霜は
　　　　創りだしている静寂を。暖炉からは聞こえてくる
　　コオロギの歌声が、暖かくいや増しにあたたかく
　　　聞き惚れて人は物憂げになるほどだ
　　　　草茂る丘にはキリギリスも鳴いているのだから

　ソネッツ「キリギリスとコオロギ」"On the Grasshoppers and Crickets" における、セステット部分の引用。キリギリスとコオロギ（夏—冬）の鳴き声の連続性（コンティニュイティ）を歌っている。何れも日没にうたいはじめる。キリギリスは月桂樹と同じアポロにとって神聖なもの[3]である。うたの連続性は "evergreen" に通じる。
　大地ばかりでない。海原にも詩（うた）がある。「神秘の声をもつ海に／耳傾けるひとはみな／来しかた行く末をつらつら考えるに違いない」"The ocean with ~ /Its voice mysterious, which whoso hears/Must think on what will be, and what has been." (*To My Brother George*, 5–8)。大地、せせらぎ、湖、海、天地・自然すべてが一日の終わりには、夕暮れの階調を奏でる。

So the unnumber'd sounds that evening store;

The songs of birds—the whisp'ring of the leaves—

神話と現実——キーツ詩におけるアポロ

The voice of waters—the great bell that heaves
　　With solemn sound,—and thousand others more,
That distance of recognizance bereaves,
　　Make pleasing music, and not wild uproar.

　　　　　　　　　　　　　　"How many birds" (9–14)

こうして無数の旋律が夕暮れを用意する
　　小鳥の歌声——木々の葉の囁き——
海原のざわめき——高く聞こえる時鐘
　　その厳かさ——さらなる無数の旋律
距離感のないそこはかなさが
　　楽しい調べとなり　耳に心地よい

　　　　　　　　「いかに多くの詩人たちが——」(9–14)

　アポロは大地、海原を支配する。彼がダフネを追いかけた舞台は地上天——テムペの谷。彼はまたパルナッソスの山で9人の詩神たちとよく踊り戯れていた（パンが美しいニンフたちを追うのは天上地アルカディア）。キーツ詩にはつねに天と地の交流があった。緑の丘で／我ら心ゆくまで味わう／黄金色の陽光を／脳味噌が混じり合うまで／アポロの栄光に輝く優美さに（「ソング」12-6）。

　アポロは光。思想、情念、感性、知性のエッセンスという意味で、詩は詩人の精神、魂の光である。ぶどうは秋の収穫。四季の陽光をいっぱい浴びた、熟れたぶどうの実。「ああ一杯の

第 1 部

ぶどう酒が欲しい！／花の女神と緑の野原／収穫祭の踊り　プロヴァンス地方の恋の唄　陽に焼けた歓楽を味わった一杯のぶどう酒が」「ナイティンゲールの賦」(11-5) という語が口を衝いてでて来る。ワインは正にアポロ神に祝福されたぶどうのエセンスそのもの。「ソング」はアポロの光、詩、ワインが一体となって、溶け合う芳醇な美を歌う。同時に、この詩は魂の成熟を暗示する。知、成熟への旅を繰り返し奏でる豊かさがここにある。

　キーツはクラアレットを好む。ワインの微少な酔いは脳神経を刺激する。詩はあたまで創りりだすものではない。絶えず情緒情感という土壌から生命力がむくむく芽をだし、伸びようとする。その動きを瞬間に捉え、己の内面の真実を歌わずにいられなくなる。思想は経験・知識・感性によって紡がれる。軽度のワインは触媒。クラアレットは「天の古酒」にも通じるエキスであったに違いない。

　さて彼がワーズワシアンである友人のベイリー宛の書簡の一節を引用したい、

　　　「複雑な心の持ち主——想像力が豊かで、その果実についても細心の注意を払う人——彼は感覚と思索の両方に生きようとするが、そういう人には、必然的に歳月が物の道理を弁える心をもたらせてくれるものだ——君はそういう心の持ち主とぼくは思う。だから君が永遠の幸福をうるためには、地上の最も精妙な瞑想とぼくが呼ぶこの天の古酒を飲むばかりでなく、知識をふやすこと、あらゆることを

知ることが必要なのだ[4]

　天の古酒は、感覚と知性（思索）を通しての想像力を意味している。ここに知性は情念を乳首とし、現世から苦悩、矛盾を吸いとり、人間は成長するという、「魂創造」寓話──を萌芽のカタチで読みとることができよう。
　ところで、N・プーサン (Poussin, Nicolas, 1594–1665) に、「詩人の霊感」（ルーヴル美術館）がある。詩神たちを従えているアポロから、詩人が霊感を授かる構図。月桂樹の根元の床几に腰かけているアポロ。左手に竪琴、それを右腕の太い部分に凭せかけ、右手の人さし指で何か詩人に指図している。彼は月桂冠をあたまに戴く。詩人は右手に鵞ペン、左手に羊皮紙。それらは左の膝で支えられている。眼は天の一隅を凝視。両者を隔てる空間には、キューピッドが舞い、愛の使者も両手にそれぞれ月桂冠をもつ。そして、左手にもつそれをいま正に詩人のあたまに載せようとしている。正面の左にもう一人キューピッド。右手に月桂冠をもつ。背後にミューズが一人侍り、アポロの仕草をじっと見つめる。時刻は夕暮れか？　霊感には神性が宿る。永遠性を分かち合うアポロとキーツ。両者の「共謀（する）」"conspire"（「秋」）は、詩人究極の意図であろう。

　　そうだ　空しい生を捨て高貴な人生を生きなければならない
　そこでぼくはあらゆる苦しみ　人間の心の苦悩を見いだす

第 1 部

　　であろう
　何故なら見るがいい！　ぼくは眼にするのだから　彼方に
　碧く突き出た岩を超え　たてがみ棚引かせ　馬車をひく
　疾走する駿馬たちを──操る御者は見つめている
　栄光に満ちてはいるが恐ろしげな風の力を

　　　　……………………………

　ヴィジョンはみな消え失せた──馬車は天空の
　光の中に消え　ヴィジョンの代わりに
　物事の実在感覚が倍の力強さで訪れる
　そして濁流さながら　ぼくの魂を押し流し　追いやるのだ
　無へと　ぼくはあらゆる疑惑と戦い
　馬車と　それが辿っていった
　不思議な旅路に思いを馳せたい　（『眠りと詩』123–162）

感覚から思索へ。この魂の成熟プロセスにおいても、キーツは
つねに感覚の瑞々しい生命力を忘れていない。ここにキーツ詩
の魅力がある。霊感によって大空に描きだされる、馬車を操る
アポロの辿る軌跡と思索。感覚の翳りはつねに未来を暗示する。
　キーツ詩の中心軸は、『眠りと詩』、『エンディミオン』、『ハ
イピリオン』、「没落」の叙事詩群と、6篇のオード群。『イザ
ベラ』、『聖アグネス祭前夜』、『レイミア』の物語詩群。それら
の間隙を埋めるソネッツ、書簡体詩群。さらに抒情詩、妖精
詩、断片詩群となる。『書簡集』に、これら全てを包含す

12

る詩論が展開されている。つらぬく強烈なイメージは、知識への切ないほどの憧れ、吸収欲であり、不断の現実意識。ファニー・ブローンへの愛、さらに人類愛である。結核に病む愛——かなしい若さに、真善美への憧憬の全てが溢れ、そこにアポロの放つ "golden color" があり、詩、医学、予言、音楽などアポロの諸機能がオーガニックに統一され、自らを重ねる。

(3)

　キーツ詩の魅力の一つは、ギリシャ神話を自家薬籠中のものとしている点にある。『エンディミオン』がそうだ。アポロの妹・シンシア。そしてパンは、オルフェウス視点（宇宙的、普遍的）で描かれている。アポロとパンは交錯。アポロがジョーヴの不興を蒙り、天国から追放され、テッサリーで牧羊者になったとき、彼はパンに音楽のてほどきを試みたという。黄金時代は去り、偉大なるパンは死んだ。その姿は奇妙なものであった。

　　「角は太陽の光、あるいは新月を表し、その赤ら顔は一
　　日の軌道のイメージを、身にまとう豹の皮は、星空のシン
　　ボルである。下半身の毛深い姿は、通常は灌木、むぎ、草
　　に覆われている大地の肥沃性を表す」[5]

パンが天空、大地を象徴していることは普遍性、宇宙性を意味

第1部

する。琴の名手オルフェウス。彼の奏でる旋律は全ての生きも
の、川、樹木、小石までも歓ばせた。普遍性とオルフェウスが
同一視される所以である。

『エンディミオン』の基底に「パン讃歌」(l. 247–306) がある。
エロティシズムで貫かれている。

　　　——幸福はどこにあるのか？　それは
　　ぼくらの準備のできた心を　実在する美との交わりに
　　招きよせることの中にある　こうして遂にぼくらは輝き
　　充分に変容を遂げ　空間を自由に駆けめぐる

　　　……………………………

　　　　　そのときぼくらは
　　いわば過去現在未来の一元的世界に足踏み入れ
　　ただよう霊の状態になる　だがそこには
　　自己否定などでは到達しえないいっそう豊かな
　　心を捉え心を奪うものがある　それがぼくらの心を
　　じょじょに最高の強烈性にみちびいていく

　　　……………………………

　　　　　けっきょく
　　その輝きのなかに溶けて　ぼくらは交わり
　　混じり合って　その輝く光の一部となる

神話と現実——キーツ詩におけるアポロ

ここは「幸福論」のさわりの部分である。「実在する美（本質）との交わり」"A fellowship with essence" は、結局、エンディミオンとシンスイアとの抱擁を意味している。全てを認め許し、契りを結べば、愛するもの同士は、心もからだも光り輝く。充分に変容をとげることになる。漂う霊の状態となり、その輝きの中に溶け、交わり、混じり合って、その輝く光の一部となる。

　人は幸福に憧れる。夢中にさせてくれるものが欲しい。自然、芸術、友情。彼は友情を通し、広く人類愛に目覚める。詩人の想像力は素直に、己の身の周りから羽ばたく。言うところの「悦びの温度計」"pleasure thermometer" も、「幸福論」を一読すれば納得できる。キーツはこのとき、真実 (truth) に対し、想像力の規則正しい足取りを感じていた。現実の悲哀に眼をむける心のゆとりと必然性が、想像力を羽ばたかせる。想像力は、現実を一つの劇として迫る。(6) そして、Negative Capability によって現実を把握する。

　　　つねに酵母菌であれ
　　この活力のない土塊の大地に広がり
　　大地に霊妙なる接触を――新たなる生誕を与えるパン種で
　　あれ　（第 1 巻）(296–298)

5 連からなるパン讃歌の中心思想はこの 3 行に収斂される。
　ところで、「霊妙なる（天空の、エーテル状の）」"ethereal" という語、およびアントニウムの「素材、物質」"material" は、

15

第 1 部

キーツ詩のキーワードの一つ。すなわち、素材がエーテル状になる想像力形成の発展過程において、"distill–distillation"、"intensify–intensity"、"abstract–abstraction"、"digest–digestion"、"evaporate–evaporation"、"sublime–sublimation" など、医学に関する化学実験の用語が関係してくる。素材に加熱すると、しだいにイシアリアルな状態に近づく。不純分子がエヴァポレイトし、最後に "essence"、"spirit"、"etherealization" の状態となる。1816 年 7 月 25 日に彼は、当時、時代の最先端をいく、近代化されたガイ・ホシピタルにおいて外科医の資格を習得している。

さて、情熱、創造、生殖の根源であるパンは、詩・予言・霊感を司るアポロと多くの点で通底し、重層する。アポロはまたシンスイア（ダイアナ、ヘカテ）とも重なる。『ハイピリオン』、「没落」の主役、記憶の女神・ニーモジニー、モネタには、キーツの想像力が宿る。アポロ・キーツとも重なり、原点に『エンディミオン』がある。

愛の讃歌『エンディミオン』。この詩の前半に歌われる生命の胚胎と再生は、パン讃歌の流れの中にあり、地水火風の構成を支える。アポロは昼間の光。シンスイアは夜の光。陽と陰、動と静。地水火風は生命力につらぬかれ、昼夜の別なし。前半 200 行は、パン讃歌、幸福論（第 1 巻）、アドニス神話、幻の恋の成就、アルフェウスとアリシューザ（第 2 巻）の神話構成になっている。

前半と後半を重ねる伏線として、妹ピオナの果たす役割は大きい。"Peona" の根源に "Paean"「讃歌、アポロへの祈願のうた」。"Paean=Paeon"。"Paeon"「ギ神・パイエオン」は、オリ

16

神話と現実——キーツ詩におけるアポロ

ンパスの神々に医師として仕えた神。後、アポロと同一視される。"son of Apollo" [7] と考えられる。さらに、"Paeon" が薬草 (Paeoniae herbae) に由来を知ると、詩人の意図が推察できよう。治療者、医師はつねに愛と光の使者。後半のヒューマニテ
$\overset{ヒーラー}{治療者}$、$\overset{フィジシアン}{医師}$はつねに愛と光の使者。後半のヒューマニテアリアリズムへの移行の準備は密かになされている。

さらに「幸福の段階説」に先立つこと2カ月、ベイリー宛の手紙[8]において、「想像力の真実に関するぼくの気に入りの思索」と称し、「幸福論」と「悲しみの歌」についての言及がある。両者の不可分性は、詩人の命題であった。この手紙はちょうど「第3巻」執筆中に書かれた。

「第3巻」は「悲しみの歌」(第4巻) にいたるプロセス。ここには友情と愛による現実開眼が語られている。幸福論第3段の前半には友情の側面がある。「第3巻」の中心テーマは「グローカス神話」。悲劇が感動をもって歌われる。悲哀に込められているのは美であり、輝かしい美と同様に心を感動させる。心の感動は神聖なもの。激しい情熱は愛と同じであり、この情熱が高められ、荘厳な状態になると美そのものを創りだすからである。エンディミオンとシンスイアとの「幻の恋の成就」は、いわば、「一元的世界に足を踏み入れ／(ぼくらは) 漂う霊の状態になる」瞬間の到来であり、そのとき「人類への眼覚めた共感を覚える」ことになる。この人道的博愛主義は、「アルフェウスとアリシューザ」における、二人の実を結ばぬ恋ゆえの激しい苦悩にみちた訴えのさ中、「共に天駆けよう／この侘しい洞窟から無現の大空めざして」(End., II. 986–7) と、詩人がアルフェウスに言わせる言葉と響き合う。この部分も「霊化」

17

第1部

（第4巻）の伏線である。感覚（性の交わり）による形而上的
世界の理解は、つねに思想の翼に新しい活力を与える[9]にある。
このプロセスに「グローカス神話」の意義がある。友情と愛に
よる人道主義的博愛主義への回心。エンディミオンの分身・グ
ローカスの貢献は、「歓喜と悲哀という人間に負わされた課業」
(End. III. 702) である。この課業は三つの「讃歌」（フィービー、
ネプチューン、キューピッド）に守られ、成就の方向にむか
う。真実を象徴するシラを廻る現実回帰。逃避ではない。帰す
るところ再生、創造。ここにもアポロ（天空）とシンスイアの
視点が息づいている。

　地、水をつらぬくパッション・火。パッションの実体はエン
ディミオン。彼は、「第4巻」の「風」を支配する女神・シン
スイアに憧れつつも、姿見せずに歌声だけ聞いて印度少女に恋
してしまう。彼女は大地の象徴。したがって彼女への愛は、他
者への愛を意味し、「グローカス神話」の延長線上に捉えられ
る。歓喜はつねに悲哀と表裏。現実は一瞬のエクスタシー、フ
ァローン。紆余曲折をへて、彼は「静謐の洞窟」(End., iv. 512–
62) に沈潜する。そこはいわば、美が真に生まれ変わるところ。
魂創造のミニ版、さきがけ。生死の境界線を彷徨う厳しい試練
をへて、彼はふたたび地上に戻る。狭義のエゴは払拭された。
いわば大いなるセルフの誕生。彼は幸福の最終段階に到達す
る。夢を捨て、乙女さえ見限ったこの瞬間、印度少女はシンス
イアに変容。二人は抱擁し、天空の彼方に姿を消す。

　「霊化」（心身の合体）(ibid, iv. 993) は行われた。不純物は蒸留
され、化学実験でいえばエセンス、酒精（スピリツ）だけがエーテル状に残

ることになる。だがこの霊化に唐突性が残る限り、不自然であり、本物でない。季節が訪れ、樹木に葉が生い茂るように自然に、美が真になるのでなければ、その作品は理想詩といえない。『エンディミオン』は未熟である。したがって、擬似「霊化」から、二つのハイピリオンにおける、本殿の「真理の階段」を登りつめようとするアポロ・キーツの姿が浮かぶ。アイデンティティ追求の旅は、モネタ（ニーモジニー）の蒼白な顔を覆うヴェールが取り除かれるまでつづく。

(4)

　「ぼくはあまり遅くならない内に、美しいギリシャ神話に手を染め、その光輝を汚したい。なぜなら、ギリシャ神話と訣別するまえに、もう一度、挑戦したいからだ。」（序文）多くの可能性を秘めている『エンディミオン』。『ハイピリオン』、「没落」は、その未熟さを補完し、大きく踏み出した作品。主人公は、啓示に従って、運命を切り拓いていこうとする。タイタン族の凋落は、黄金時代の終わり、偉大なるパンの死、アダムとイヴの楽園追放、時間の始まりなどの背景を考えさせる。天上から追われ、地下の土牢に幽閉される巨人族の描く軌跡は、天地を駆け巡る人間の想像力のアナロジーとなる。この詩は単なる叙事詩でない。ジョーヴを廃し、王位に就いたサターンは、サツゥルヌス＝クロノス、時の神の謂いである。
　『エンディミオン』と『ハイピリオン』は、印度少女にアポロ・

第 1 部

キーツを重ねるとわかり易い。悲哀を軸として、両者は延長線上にある。シンシィアとの真の合体は、現世の悲哀（ワールド・グリーフ）の自覚であった。つまり、幸福論（自然・友情・愛）の延長線上に、ヴェイルを脱ぐモネタの姿（人類愛）を捉えうる。治療者（ヒーラー）の機能をもつアポロが重層され、予言者としての機能は、啓示と繋がる。現実の悲哀にメランコリーは胚胎し、美はいっそう輝きをます。こうしてパン讃歌、幸福論、幻の恋の成就、霊化を陽画とすれば、グローカス神話、印度少女、悲しみの歌、アポロの神格化は陰画となる。両者を合わせると理想詩の枠組みができる。接点にメランコリーがあり、アポロ像が全体を統括する。

　二つのハイピリオンは繋がっている。だが何故、「没落」なのか？　タイタン神族は黄金時代を生きてきた。だが時代が変わって、時を刻む時代が訪れた。無傷のハイピリオンの静かなる退場は、巻き戻しの利かない、時代の変化を意味し、キーツ自身の精神的成熟と重なる。

　さて宇宙の政権交代の神話劇において、敗北し、追放される旧世代に属するタイタン神族の苦しむ姿に、詩人は己の精神的葛藤と現世の苦しみを見る。それの概念化、巨人族敗北の原因追究。詩人の態度はきわめて理性的、知的である。3巻からなる『ハイピリオン』を概観しよう。

　「第1巻」にはタイタン神族の敗北後の苦しむ様子が描かれている。全体の基調は荘重（サブライム）であり、サターンの描写に関して著しい (1–14)。近づいてきたテアの姿も荘重かつ彫刻的 (26–30)[10]。興味ふかいのは、ガイ病院おける手術室の光景[11]を想像させる描写である。たとえば、「彼は両手を虚空にもがかせ／〜汗を

にじませ／両眼を見開き声は途絶えた」(136–38)。「つま先から頭のてっぺんまで／巨大な彼の全身に苦悶が緩やかに這いのぼった」(259–60) など。前後するが、「心臓に痛みを感じたりする」(42–4) 光景もある。病院の手術室を連想させる光景は「第2巻」にいってもつづく。

　　（彼らは）食いしばった歯をなおもきしませながら
　　暗闇の土牢に投げこまれたり　四肢はみな
　　太い針金のようにねじ曲げられ　ぎっしり詰め込まれてい
　　　た
　　そこは大きな胸が　苦痛にふくらむ以外は身動きもならず
　　彼らはただ衝動的に　血が沢山ほとばしり
　　恐ろしくけいれんするばかりだった　　(23–8)

　「第二巻」の特徴は苦痛の概念化である。ここに登場し、発言する主だった神々は、サターン、先見の明のある賢者オーシアナス、直観力鋭いクリミニー、気骨ある主戦論者エンセラダス。それぞれが自ら信じ、直観的に感じ、意識しているところを述べるのだが、「この議論の背景には、古典的なシンポジウムの伝統がある。ここで各自は感応し、他を拒絶せずに、全ての意見を完結させる。たとえ全員一致でなくても、少なくとも共通の理想にむかって会議をすすめる」(12)。この「古典的なシンポジウムの伝統」の意味は、キーツのいう「ギリシャ的様式」と重なり、『饗宴』のエコーである。具体的な個々の苦痛は「真理の苦痛」"the pain of truth" (Hyperion II. 202) に収斂さ

21

第1部

れ、概念化される。「ありのままの真実に耐えること／そして
冷静そのものに現実を正視すること／これが最高の力」(203-5)
と、じゅんじゅん論す、オーシアナスの理のある正論が、主戦
論、あくなき抵抗を試みようと口説くエンセラダスを、結果的
には納得させる。この場合、いわゆる「シンポジウム」(饗宴)
形式の、神々の激論の流れを変える大きな役割を果たすのが、
サターンの娘、クリミニーの「ありのままの声」コトバ "the simplest
voice" (252)。

　彼女は味方に利のないことを肌で感じ、悦びのときは終わっ
たことを知る。そのとき彼女は、「芳香漂う／静寂な　樹木茂
り　花々咲き乱れる内陸から／甘い空気が吹きよせる楽しい岸
辺」(262-4) にいた。「悦楽と快い暖かさが満ちみちていた」
(266) にもかかわらず、その歓びを彼女は「惨めなうた　悲し
みの音楽」 "songs of misery, music of our woes" (269) で否定し
ようとする。このとき新鮮な「幸満てる黄金色の旋律」 "new
blissful golden melody" (280) が聞こえてくる。この音楽はアポ
ロの到来を告げる前触れであるが、クリミニーを印度少女の延
長線上に捉えることも決して無理であるまい。

　「第3巻」の主役はアポロ・キーツ。だが、彼は未だ経験不
足であり、精神的にも未熟であるから、「詩歌の父」 "the
Father of all verse" (13) として充分に振る舞うことはできない。
神性ゴッドヘッドの支配をうけるこころ準備も整っていないから、彼のう
たごえには、「ドーリアのフルートの爽やかな旋律」 "soft warble
from the Dorian flute" (12) の伴奏を従える程度である。「畏れを
知らぬ痛々しい程の純情」 "aching ignorance" (107) は正されね

22

神話と現実──キーツ詩におけるアポロ

ばならない。それには経験が不可欠となる。宇宙的に重要な問題は、未だ詩にうたえない。いま目の前で行われている利のない戦、オーシアナスの卓見、クリミニーの鋭い洞察力なども含め、「おびただしい知識がわたしを神にさせる」"Knowledge enormous makes a God of me" (113) と彼はいう。だがこの知識は現実の苦しみを通して得られた英知ではない。

容赦ない苛酷な現実の受容、現実感覚の深化。これらがしだいにこの叙事詩に姿を現してくる。オーシアナスのストイックな主張は、己の非力をすすんで認めよというにある。人間は精神的に成長しなければ、現実の真の様相は見えてこない。知識の吸収は、厳しい試練に耐え、はじめて生命を帯びてくる。アポロは一歩、踏みこみ、悲哀は創造的という認識を示す。彼は悲哀に対し、「個人的な理由によってではなく、人類のそれとして受け止める。こうして彼は神になる」[13]。己を客観化し、他者への愛に生きること。そこに神が宿るが、いまのアポロは物いわぬニーモジニーの顔をじっと見つめている。このとき、彼の魂の内部で夢想家の要素である主観的自我と、「真の詩人」の要因である客観的自我が火花を散らせていた。なぜなら、「第3巻」は難行苦行の末、中断されるからである。

愛弟トマスの死は、キーツにとって、耐えられない程の試練であった。心の襞、微妙なキーツの起伏屈折する心理状況に理解のあったかけ替えのないトムの存在。キーツの悲しみの慟哭が聞こえてくる行間に、「没落」が胚胎する。「第3巻」は、1819.1～4月某日まで謎の沈黙の1カ月を含め、幾たびか中断しながら、書き続けられた。僅か130行。だが要した日数の多

第 1 部

さは異常である。

　ニーモジニー。「彼女は、人間の歴史的ヴィジョンと、理解の擬人化されたものであり、歴史の変化と、人間の条件そのものに備わる本来的な、避けられない苦悩を映しだす鏡である。」[(14)]つまり、アポロが物いわぬニーモジニーの顔から、学びとる生きた知識、博愛精神、それが彼を神に昇華させる。アポロの神格化は、いうなれば "God-making" である。この思考方式は、1819.4.21 日付けのジョージ・キーツ夫妻宛の書簡に認められた、「魂創造」寓話と軌を一にする。

　ニーモジニーは、ある意味において、詩人の想像力が生みだした存在であり、「来るべき現実の影」であることを考えるとき、現実の苦しみに対し、乏しい経験の裏打ちしかない彼には、無言の彼女の顔から読みとる「おびただしい知識」は刺激であり、魅力であった。女神の神格がしだいに乗り移ってくるプロセスに、未熟な「本質との交わり」を、深化させようとする真剣な姿勢がみられる。概念的知識から、他者への愛の自覚による真の知識（英知）への成熟である。――「すると激しい震えが彼を襲い／神さびて美しい四肢を燃えたたせたが／それは死に臨んだときの苦悶にあまりにもよく似ていた／あるいは蒼白な永遠の死に訣別れ(わか)を告げ／死の激痛の悪寒と同じくらいに熱い激痛と激しいけい攣を伴って／生まれ変わる人間にいっそうよく似ていた」(124–130)。

　こうして「第三巻」は中断される。「魂創造」寓話と、時期的に一致する。行き詰まりを打開すべく、「没落」と題し、衣替えし、「夢」形式の「歌」(Canto) として書き続けられる。ミ

24

ルトン的手法では、成熟しつつあったキーツの思想はもはや表現しえないと、実感したのである。背後に、トマスの死の影響が影を落としている。執筆は八月。1819 年の春は彼の天才の華ひらくアナス・ミラビリスであった。六篇の賦と妖精詩『レイミア』に「没落」、「秋」となる。この間の 2、3 の書簡に注目したい。三月半ば過ぎから、四月下旬にかけて、ジョージ・キーツ夫妻宛のものだ。

> 「──ぼくがテンの機敏さとか鹿の不安の様子を見るとき感じるように、遥か高い存在が、ぼくの心のとる本能的に優美な態度をみて、楽しむということはないであろうか？　街の通りの喧嘩は好ましくないが、その中に見られるエネルギーは素晴らしい。どんなにありふれた人間でも、喧嘩になると優美さを発揮する──遥か高い存在からみれば、我々の頭で考えることも、これと同じようなものかも知れない。誤りだらけだが、素晴らしいというように──詩が存在するのは正にそこなのだが、もしそうだとすれば、詩は哲学ほど素晴らしいものではない──"神聖なる哲学はなんと魅力のあるものか／〜／アポロの竪琴の如く調べゆたかだ──"──何ものも経験されなければ現実のものにはならない──」[15]

「遥か高い存在」と「小さな人間」、「ポエトリー」と「喧嘩」の対比。ここに、小さな人間の枠を超えようとする詩人の姿勢がみられる。小さな人間の営む喧嘩は、多少、ぶざまなところ

第1部

があるとしても、自然発生のエネルギーは賛美に値する。彼は迸りでる根源的な力の中に自然神をみる。高い視点からすれば、喧嘩、人間などは小さく、罪のない可愛いいものだと言いたいのであろう。いっぽう、「哲学」に対する評価が高いが、彼のいう哲学は、「物の道理」と解釈したい。なぜなら、「物の道理」は、失敗を踏まえた、現実経験によって身につくからである。さらに彼は現実に透徹し、自らの詩を「遥か高い存在」に近づけようとする。詩に「真理のイメージ」"an image of truth"[16] を羽ばたかせようとする。「ものの道理＝真理」である哲学を、彼は神聖視する。アポロの奏でる旋律と同格にみようとする姿勢に、彼のいう理想詩を読みとることができよう。この書簡の約1カ月後、下記の手紙がある。

　「人間というものは元来、"あわれな二本足の生き物"で、森の動物とおなじ様々な不幸に翻弄され、それなりの困難や不安を免れない運命を負わされている。肉体の環境順応性、楽しさ加減が徐徐に訪れてくるとしても、——その程度がよくなるにつれ、実は新たな多くの苦悩が待ちうけている——人間は死ぬ運命にあるが、頭上にはいつも星の輝く天空がある。——、一体、人間はどれくらい幸福になりうるのか——幸福のいきつく先は何か——それは死だ——そういう状態に幸福がおかれている場合、誰が死に耐えられようか——我々の場合、しばしの生のあいだに少しずつ経験している労苦の全て、それは生存の最後の日まで蓄積されるのだが、それらが一度に押し寄せてくることにな

神話と現実——キーツ詩におけるアポロ

る。——ぼくはこのような幸福の完全性はまったく信じない。——この世の中の本質がそういうものの存在を許さないのだ——この世に生きる人々は世の中そのものに順応して生きるものだ——」(17)

　ここには、この世の中の本質が語られている。若さゆえの生に対する悩み、幸福をきわめることの儚さ。現実を見つめる眼差しの鋭さ。如何なる状況におかれようと、頭上には星の輝く天空があるという魂の救済。這いつくばっても、宇宙、地水火風の本質を見極めようとする詩人の眼差し。この世の中は、起伏混沌の現実である。だが仰ぎみれば星の輝く天空がある。地—天、動—静の二元世界の展開。そこに救いがある。

　完全な幸福などありえないし、死は必ず訪れる。幸福であればある程、現世に執着する。人間は二本足の動物。苦悩の絶えることはない。苦しみに意義を見いだそうとするキーツ。彼の詩の深さはそこに胚胎する。「魂創造」寓話、現世を観じる思考方式に、苦難に立ち向かおうとする詩人の積極姿勢がみられる。

　「第3巻」末尾のクライマックスは、アポロの神格化のみならず、詩人みずからのなかに人類の苦しみを受け入れ、受容させている。アポロとキーツが重ねられる所以である。それには、偏狭な己の殻を脱却し、無私の客観性を身につけねばならない。知性を鍛え、魂に仕上げるに現世の苦しみは不可欠となる。試練の耐え方に、人間の真の成長が問われることになる。他者の苦しみを自らのものとし、痛みを分かち合い自らが受容

27

第1部

する態度。それは「暗い廊下」"dark passage" を渡って、「第3室」に入ろうとしている己の詩心の展開にほかならない。アポロがつねに彼を先導する。アポロの竪琴の奏でる黄金の音色と哲学を同じレベルで考えるとき、「第3巻」と「没落」の相違がいっそう明らかになるのでないか。「没落」において、アポロは益々その姿を現してくる。

(5)

「没落」の冒頭、夢想家の未熟な感覚に共感を示しながらも、両者の相違、識別に言及。真の詩人の抱負を語るキーツ (1–18)。つづく楽園の描写は、己の苦悩を経て、いずれ「真」に昇華させねばならない想像力の描く感覚美──「美」の世界である。

Methought I stood where trees of every clime
Palm, myrtle, oak, and sycamore, and beech,
With Plantane, and spice blossoms, made a screen;
In neighbourhood of fountains, by the noise
Soft-showering in mine ears; and, by the touch
Of scent, not far from roses. Turning round,
I saw an arbour with a drooping roof
Of trellis vines, and bells, and larger blooms,
Like floral censers swinging light in air;

神話と現実——キーツ詩におけるアポロ

Before its wreathed doorway, on a mound
Of moss, was spread a feast of summer fruits,
Which nearer seen, seem'd refuse of a meal
By Angel tasted, or our Mother Eve;
For empty shells were scattered on the grass,
And grape stalks but half bare, and remnants more,
Sweet smelling, whose pure kinds I could not know.
Still was more plenty than the fabled horn
Thrice emptied could pour forth, at banqueting
For Proserpine return'd to her own fields,
Where the white heifers low. And appetite
More yearning than on earth I ever felt
Growing within, I ate deliciously;　　(19–40)

　わたしは棕櫚　天人花　樫　無花果　ブナの樹など
あらゆる風土の樹木が　プラタナスや匂い妙なる花と一緒
　　に
屏風を拵えている場所に佇んでいる気がした
近くには泉があり　音の
やさしく時雨れる気配をこころに聞き　複郁とした
仄かな匂いで薔薇の咲くのを知る。見回すと
垂れ下がったあずまやの屋根の
四つ目格子の棚に葡萄が絡み　風鈴草や大きめの花が
花の香炉さながら　風のなか軽やかに揺れていた
花輪で飾られた扉口の前の苔むす丘の上に

第 1 部

　　　夏の果実の饗宴が繰り広げられていた
　　　近寄って見るとそれは天使か　母なるイヴが
　　　味わい食べた食事の残りらしかった　そう思うのも
　　　空の外皮　半分剝きだしの葡萄の茎
　　　沢山の残り屑　まこといかなる種類か見当もつかない
　　　甘い匂いのするものが草の上に散らばっていたからだ
　　　そこには白い仔牛が啼く
　　　故郷の野畑に戻ったプロサパインを迎える饗宴のとき
　　　三たび傾けられた　思いのまま果実など打ちだせる伝説の
　　　角杯が注ぎうるより　なお多くのご馳走があった　だから
　　　生まれて初めての何ともいえぬ食欲がこみあげ
　　　わたしは舌鼓を打って食べた　(19–40)

　ここには、あずまや、自然、処女思想の部屋、夢想家、楽園、
追放以前のイヴの姿が投影している。その裏で聖域、芸術、暗
い通路、真の詩人、現世、苦悩するモネタが息づく。この
"locus amoenus"（魅力ある場所）[18] は、オード群の世界に通底
する側面をもつ。
　すなわち、「インドレンス」における、「花々、揺れる影、挫
折する微光の振り撒かれた芝草」、「サイキ」における、キュー
ピッドとサイキの寄り添う芝生と重なる。「ナイティンゲール」
では、花々咲き乱れる薄暗がりの理想郷。「甕」にあっては、
色褪せない男女の彫刻模様のフリーズに。さらに歓喜と悲哀の
溶け合う「メランコリー」も加わる。つまり、Odes 群の主人
公はみなこの序文の "bower" の住人と無関係でないといえる。

その上、視覚（棕櫚、天人花、樫、無花果、ブナの樹、プラタナス）、聴覚（泉の音）、嗅覚（薔薇の匂い）、味覚（夏の果実の饗宴）、また触覚とも響き合う。五感に訴える情感と知性は、絶えず錯綜し、『ハイピリオン』における非時間世界（サターン＝サトゥルヌス黄金時代）、意識に刻まれる時間（サターン失脚以後）の時代、両者の葛藤を喚起させる。

「想像力が美として捉えたものは真」の視点からは、「美」の「真」への変容に、詩人の苦悩が求められる。感覚の充足が、詩人を限りなくヴィジョナリーにさせる。飽くなき知識の吸収と現世の悲哀経験。詩人は他者への愛の化身になろうと努力する。アポロに己を「新鮮な生贄」"a fresh sacrifice"（『眠りと詩』61）として捧げているキーツ。モネタの苦悶は詩人のそれである。

続いてひとつのセレモニー。「地上の全ての人々や　その名がなお／我らの口を賑わすあらゆる死者のため」(44-5) の「乾杯」。儀式としての乾杯は過去（『エンディミオン』の未熟）を弔い、前途（いま書き続ける詩）を祝する意味」[19]。「心ゆくばかりの美酒はわが詩の主題の生みの親」"That full draught is parent of my theme" (46) となる。「昏睡」"the cloudy swoon" (55) は、キーツ得意とする手法。

ひたすら知識を求めて止まなかったキーツ。吸収した知識の、経験を通した己の内的成熟によって、「情念」と「知性」、「魂」と「精神」の確執は薄れ、両者は融合し、祝福された心の平和が訪れる（「秋」）。

ところで、「死んで甦る」("die into the life") 光景が、『ハイピリオン』「第三巻」(124-130) と「没落・1」(122-132) の両方に描

第 1 部

かれている。何処が異なるのか？　前者は受け身、後者は、能動（階段を登る）姿勢[20]と言えないか。

　　死の一分前にわたしの凍りついた足は階段の最下段に触れ
　　　た
　　足が階段に触れると生命が足のつま先から
　　流れこんでくる気がした　　(132-4)

　「乾杯」─「昏睡」─「死んで甦る」─「階段」。「かつて美しい天使たちが／梯子伝いに大地から天へ昇ったように／わたしも登って」("I mounted up,/As once fair Angels on a ladder flew/From the green turf to heaven.) (134-6) いく。ここは天に通じるヤコブの階段への連想。モネタのいる場所は、横臥するサターンが背景（第 1 歌、234-8）。この 2 人はかつて楽園の住人。先の引用の 10～13 行目「夏の果実の饗宴」に打興じた天使たちと、微妙に響き合う。

　何故に、無傷のハイピリオンが没落するのか？時の経過は、いっそう充実した「普遍的な美と調和をもつ慈悲深い神」(21) を必要とした。部分から全体・普遍へ、個から綜合へ。詩人の天才の急速な成長が裏にある。

　「没落」は、醒めた夢の中で憧れに悶えながら、魂の知覚するヴィジョンを描く。翼をえて天空を飛翔したいキーツ。Moneta = Memory, Juno。モネタはハイペリオンとともに、タイタン族最後の生き残りで、不変の非時間に生きる慈悲の神。女神の顔は月光の彩色、黙示録的。モネタは、月（癒し）とも繋がる

神話と現実——キーツ詩におけるアポロ

("The Fall", l. 268–71)。更に、思想、思索も司る。[22]

　記憶を軸にすると、キーツにおいてシンシアは、モネタと重なる。いわば前身。『エンディミオン』、『ハイピリオン』、「没落」の要約は、主人公の光への旅となる。「知識の極限」は光。幼いときから己を光と結び付けようとしていたキーツ。モネタの頭蓋骨の内側における悲劇の内容は、過去・現在・未来に通じる歴史、真理、光である。現世の変化を映しとる永遠。究極の慈悲でもある。

　キーツは、己のコトバで永遠を語ろうとする。吸収する知識から、絶えず己のコトバを紡ぎだそうとする。"patient" は、彼自身の生きる姿勢。モネタにグローカス、ニオベ、シビリーさえ投影[23]していると知れば、詩人の「辛抱強さ」が理解できる。

　自然は変化する。そこには真理がある。キーツはそれを描こうとする。シェイクスピアへの傾倒である。『ハイピリオン』と「没落」は、時間世界へ転落する神々をうたう。変化。生き残るモネタ。女神は不死、永遠。アポロ＝モネタ＝キーツと重ねるとき、この叙事詩の全体像が見えてくる。

　知識を絶えず求めても、感覚を知性より優位においたキーツ。しかし、「感情の虚偽」"pathetic fallacy" は、極力避ける。意識せず、周囲に歓び、癒しを与える存在にまで、感情昇華の努力を自らに課している。四季の変化、自然のもつ永遠性を自らのコトバで表現しようとするキーツ。永遠は変わらない。キーツ詩は「無常」を超え、自然を歌おうとする。「永遠」に対する挑戦でないか。アポロを自らのものにしたい念願がそこにある。

33

第1部

　現実の日常生活を永遠の相の中に捉え、さりげなく歌うキーツ。プロサパインを響かせ、シアリーズの豊穣性に傾斜する詩人。「秋」の女神は、「アポロ―太陽」"Apollo-Sun" の「心の友」"bosom-friend" である。神話を自家薬籠中のものとしている。

　　O may no wintry season, bare and hoary,
　　See it half finished: but let autumn bold,
　　With universal tinge of sober gold,
　　Be all about me when I make an end.

"Endymion" 1, 54–57

　　おお　剥きだしで侘しい冬がくる前に
　　せめて半分は終えていたい　そして季節は秋
　　いちめん美しい黄金色であって欲しい
　　物語を書き上げる頃　ぼくの周りは

『エンディミオン』1 巻 54–57

未熟な『エンディミオン』。中断される「二つのハイピリオン」。だがキーツには一貫して、秋への憧れがある。実りの秋――黄金色の太陽。期待と凋落への恐怖。

　　O may these joys be ripe before I die.

"Sleep and Poetry". 269

　　死ぬまえにこれらの喜びが熟して欲しい

『眠りと詩』269

　　　　　　　　　　　　　　　神話と現実──キーツ詩におけるアポロ

　絶えず知識を追い求め、手に入れた知識は肉化され、精神的
成長を遂げてやまない。こうして、さりげない日常生活から、
人生の本質を穿つ輝きを見いだし、それを自らのコトバに反映
させる。そのプロセスで N. Capability が自我 "Self" を消滅させ
る。"visual" な感覚が「客観的相関物」を生みだす。感覚＝直
覚 "Sensation" が思想 (Thought) 化される。モネタ神殿の階段
を登ることが、「秋」の創作に繋がる。「没落」の中断である。

　さて「秋」に移る。要約すると、第 1 連は「結実」、「霧と甘
い果実の季節」"Season of mist and mellow fruitfulness"。第 2
連は、穀物倉の床に、もの憂げに坐り込む農婦となった秋。詩
人の眼を通した秋の「収穫」。「お前はりんご酒が、最後の一滴
まで絞りとられるのを、じっと見つめている」"Thou watchest
the last oozing hours by hours"。第 3 連は、地底から湧き出た
虫、天空から舞いおりた小鳥、神性を宿す子羊の鳴き声、黄金
色の陽射しなどを通し、紡ぎだされ、滲みでる旋律を背景に、
秋そのものの具体的な姿が描かれている。キーワードは「刈り
株畑」。「刈り株畠を薔薇色に染める」"And touch the stubble
plains with rosy hue" となる。詩人はじっと薔薇色のメロディ
に聞き入っている。

　ここには、駆り立てられるような苛立ちはない。霧も己の人
生の負のメタファではない。控え目な、秋に対する熱烈な追求
による「精神の挨拶」が繰り返され、そのプロセスにおいて「知
性」と、「震えるように繊細な、カタツムリの触角による美の
知覚」に触れる数々の詩の材料の間に生じるコトバの「無数の
構築と解体」("innumerable composition and decomposition")[24]

35

第 1 部

が繰り返され、洗練された知的なコトバが生み出されている。神話的には、ハイピリオンの娘・ルナ (Heaven) ＝ダイアナ (Earth) ＝ヘカテ／プロサパイン (Hell) の関係となる。

　感覚の思想化の実体に触れたい。第 1 連の「結実」は、第 2 連の、潰されてリンゴ酒に変化していく、果実を見つめる擬人化された秋の辛抱強い眼差しと呼応。さらに、第 3 連の「刈り株畠」の想像的余韻（娘プロサパインを地底に拉致されたシアリーズの嘆き）が、"gnats"「ブヨ」、"lamb"「子羊」、"crickets"「コオロギ」、"the redbreast"「赤い胸のコマドリ」、"swallows"「ツバメ」に繋がる連続性に注目したい。セルフを否定する洗練された知的な N. Capability による詩的表現が、魂の転生を喚起させる。虫、小動物の登場は、神話的視点を加えると、魂の輪廻を物語る。小動物がそれぞれ、精彩を帯びた「客観的相関物」となっていく。感覚の思想化である。

　ところで、キーツは、「太陽、月、星々、シェイクスピアのコトバ」＝ "real things"「リアルなもの」。「愛、雲」＝ "things semireal"「半ばリアルなもの」、さらに、イシアリアルな "no-things"「無なるもの」も、「激しい情熱」で繰り返し「精神の挨拶」を加えると、追求の激しさ故に、（詩という）実体が生みだされると考える。つづいて、「羽毛から鉄へは 3 歩の距離」("We take but three steps from feathers to iron")[25] と、謎めいたコトバを付け加える。彼の詩論を演繹すると、この場合、羽毛＝春・夏。鉄＝秋・冬と捉え得ないか？[26] 春から夏への移ろいを響かせながら、祈りをこめ、秋の停滞を歌う彼の「魂の眼覚めた痛み」は、純化され、近づく冬の訪れを感じさせる。四

季を司るアポロの微笑が伝わってくる。

　「秋」の魅力は、描きだされた地上の極楽浄土、幻の牧歌にある。死を前にした詩人のたまゆらの心の安らぎ。想像に訴える余情が、「豊穣」の「凋落」にむかう瞬間を一層美しくさせている。

　天地の恵み深い交流によって、紡ぎだされる穏やかな秋の風景。「天・地・地底」は、ハイピリオン、アポロ―ルナ、ダイアナ、ヘカテ―シンシア＝月―モネタと重なる。思想＝知性 (Apollo)。感覚・直覚 (Earth)。両者は "golden pair"[27]。天地の交流にキーツの感覚の思想化がある。凋落は意識・無意識に見え隠れしている。だがいま秋は "golden color" に輝いている。

　キーツ詩の全てはアポロの霊感、太陽神に祝福されているといえないか？　神話と内面の現実との融合。そこにキーツ詩の全てがある。

第1部

（注）

(1) Walter H. Evert, *Aesthetic and Myth in the Poetry of Keats* (Princeton, New Jersey: Princeton Univ. Press, 1965), p. 31.

(2) *The Poems of John Keats*, ed. Miriam Allott (London: Longman Group Ltd., 1970) p. 17.

(3) *Lempiere's Classical Dictionary of Proper Names mentioned in Ancient Authors Writ Large*, 3rd ed. with a short notice of Dr J. Lempiere (London: Routledge & Kegan Paul) 1984. p. 61.

(4) *The Letters of John Keats*, ed. H. E. Rollins, Vol. 1 (Cambridge, Mass: Harvard Univ. Press, 1980) p.186.

(5) Edward Baldwin, *The Pantheon* (4th ed.; London: Godwin, 1814), pp.82–83, quoted in *Keats-Shelly Journal.*, Vol. XXIX 1980, 102–103.

(6) *The Letters*, 1, 218–9.

(7) Edmund Spenser, *Faerie Queene*, III, vi, 41. cf. Walter H. Evert. *op. cit.*, p. 168.

(8) *The Letters*, 1. 184–5.

(9) Clarence D. Thorp, *The Mind of John Keats*, (New York, Oxford Univ. Press, 1926) p. 59.

(10) Ian Jack, *Keats and the Mirror of Art* (Oxford: At the Clarendon Press, 1967), pp. 164–5.

(11) Michael E. Holstein, *Keats: The Poet-Healer and the Problem of Pain.* quoted in *Keats-Shelley Journal*, Vol. XXXVI (1987), p. 44.

(12) *ibid.*, p. 46.

(13) Kenneth Muir, "The Meaning of Hyperion," *John Keats: A Reassessment* (Liverpool: Liverpool Univ. Press, 1958), p. 108.

(14) *Loc. cit.*

(15) *The Letters*, II. pp. 80–81.

(16) K. Muir., *op. cit.*, p. 110.

(17) *The Letters*, II. 101.

(18) Helen Vendler, *The Odes of John Keats* (The Belknap Press of Harvard Univ. Press, 1983), p. 208.

神話と現実――キーツ詩におけるアポロ

(19) W. H. Evert, *op. cit.*, p. 289.
(20) *ibid.*, p. 293.
(21) *ibid.*, p. 296.
(22) H. Vendler., *op. cit.*, p. 215.
(23) *ibid.*, p. 221.
(24) *The Letters*, 1. 264–5.
(25) *ibid.*, p. 243.
(26) cf. Andrew Mortion, *Keats.* (New York, Farrar Straus and Giroux, 1998), pp. 238–9.
(27) H. Vendler., *op. cit.*, p. 285.

第 2 部
Part Two

Memories and Ideas

I

Past and Present

My Biographical Sketch

I am now eighty-eight years old. I belong to the war generation. World War II ended on the 15th of August in 1945, when I was a student at Oita Economic College. While studying economics after the war, I devoted myself to agriculture for five years to help my family, because of the shortage of food.

After graduating from the College three years later than my friends, I worked as a secretary to the manager of one of the branch offices in Sankyu Transportation Company in Kitakyushu City in Fukuoka Prefecture. One year after leaving it, I found a new occupation as a teacher of bookkeeping and Soroban in Tukumi High School in Oita Prefecture. Each job was per one year. These were not for me. I could not adapt myself to the provincialism in spite of all my efforts. They only seemed to believe in money, authority and what they can see. T. S. Eliot says, "—human kind/Can-not bear very much reality." (*Four Quartets*). Moreover, J. W. von Goethe says in his *Mignion*; "only the man who knows the deep longing of his own heart, may know the anguish of one's inward heart."

By nature, I'm a man who believes in things unseen but really existing. I am particularly fond of poetry of Japan, China and European countries, and fine arts as well. I had a long cherished dream to live as what I spiritually was. Fortunately,

44

the defeat of the war gave me freedom. Our country started to live afresh. I was able to leave my birth place where I had conceived a kind of feudalistic responsibility. I had to keep our ancestor's tombs.

I came up to Tokyo with only one bag and a pure longing soul to study, and enrolled in Waseda University, the English Literature Course, the third year class, and majored in English Romantic Poetry, particularly John Keats. After finishing Graduate School in Waseda University, I got a position in Jissen Women's University in Tokyo. And eighteen years ago, I retired under the age limit.

Since then I had been quite free. I like keeping regular hours. I cannot spend any time without my favorite books. I published several books including three volumes on John Keats. Monthly I contribute an essay to *The Oita Goudou Shimbun* in my native place. It has continued for more than eighteen years. Through it, I have appreciated the communication with my "old familiar faces."

Moreover, monthly in a quiet corner of Nakamuraya Restaurant in Shinjuku, I enjoy reading English Romantic Poetry as well as Keats' poems with several old students who once attended my seminar classes.

I'm not good at writing English. By the end of this year, I plan to collect the essays written about simple daily subjects, and intend to publish them as one chapter in a privately printed book in the near future.

第 2 部

My Beloved Teacher, Homma Hisao

I walk in the early evening, softly murmuring to a beloved person in my mind. The person is none other than Dr. Homma Hisao who was my university teacher. He died thirty years ago when he was ninety-four years old.

"Sensei! Give me the time to accomplish *A Study of John Keats* (The Third Volume)", I say to him in secret.

As an authority on English Aestheticism focusing on Oscar Wilde as well as Walter Pater, he had been widely known in Japan. He was always stylish and gallant. In summer, he wore Japanese clothes: a haori, a hakama and a pair of white tabi on Japanese zori, holding an elegant folding fan in his hand. In winter, he wore an old but splendid English suit and camel-vest. He walked without a stick until the age of eighty. I was near him to the end of his days in Jissen Women's University.

He had an aesthetics all his life. I remember one episode vividly. In my university days, it was one summer afternoon when I called on him. I was slightly sweaty in a state of spiritual tension. My shoes were musty. Entering his room, I knew that incense had been burned there. He was warmhearted, spare of speech, but his words were to the point. As if there was nothing unusual, he said to me warmly and

Memories and Ideas

strictly, "Live sincerely this present moment, and it leads you to eternity."

He understood the wakeful anguish of my soul that had started from the pain of longing. He stimulated it to bring out my study into the world. His books showed me that he had never quoted second hand. His academic sentences were hard, simple and beautiful. Moreover, he was a wise expert to sum up the outline of original works. 'How to summarize a book shows what the man is.' was his lesson. Over eighty-six years old, he was asked to make speeches in public, and in the talking, now and then, he put an exquisite pause between the words. Audiences were enraptured by his speech. He was a student of Kabuki in which "a pause" always signifies something important.

"Some men with his years are like a lion; one can tell nothing of their age except they are full grown." (George Eliot). He really was one of those men and a great scholar.

The older I am, the more I want in earnest to write and read. I am proud to have been one of his students. He kept walking breezily toward an ideal world all his life. I watched him near by for thirty years long.

The season of fresh green leaves is beautiful in the evening. The setting sun reminds me of my beloved teacher.

第 2 部

A Photograph

"What? Who is that man? Is it me? Unbelievable!" I said to myself when I found a photograph between two books.

It was in a letter. The postmark on the envelope showed it had come from Hampstead, in London. The snapshot was taken before the main entrance of Keats House. I stood by the side of a new plum tree. At this place, it is said, John Keats wrote his *Ode to a Nightingale* in May 1819. Behind it spread a clump of trees. There stood a notice board on which the history of the Keats's ode was written.

The background of the snap was autumnal scenery. There were scattered fallen leaves here and there in the garden. When the winter stole on, my face looked happy and relaxed, with my black hair, erect stature, bright smile and soft expression.

It was sixteen years ago when I lived in Cambridge with the purpose of doing research on the relationship between J. Keats and European paintings and sculptures. My tutor was Dr Theodor Redpath, a scholar of John Donne as well as on Romantic Poets. He placed facilities and information at my disposal. His academic strictness stimulated me greatly. Regrettably the period of my leave was only one year.

Gazing at the photo, I felt deep remorse mixed with a

Memories and Ideas

sort of strange satisfaction that I had done my best. Hope is precarious.

The sender was an assistant curator. I remembered she was beautiful. On that day, a poets reading was held at Keats House. A small room was crowded. The picture reminded me of those pleasant days. I keenly felt my nightingale had flown away.

> Adieu! adieu! thy plaintive anthem fades,
> Past the near meadows, over the still stream,
> . . . .
> Was it a vision, or a waking dream? (75–76, 79)
> (*Ode to a Nightingale*)

I have become old rapidly because of miscellaneous things and the compromising laziness. Time passes so fast. I have lost self-confidence, youth and energy for a long while.

Now, I am perplexed about what to do with the four hundred sheets of manuscript written about Keats. I hesitate to publish the papers. I want to make the essays better. I have continued correcting ideas and wondering how best to express them. But the smile of the photo tells me "Don't worry!" The point is not in success or failure, but in the author's conscience. However old I am, the smile in the photograph is mine.

第 2 部

Newly built Gravestone

I stood on the middle of a hill belonging to the Ōtama Cemetery Park in the suburbs of Tokyo. One can see Mt. Fuji from here, if it is fine. The concrete-ground was mottled with sunbeams filtering through floating clouds. We had built here a tombstone recently for our daughter who died twenty six years ago when she was nine and a half years old. To go there, it takes about two hours from our house through JR Noborito and Tachikawa Stations. I pressed Midori's little funeral urn hard to my breast.

The sutra-chanting began. I said to myself, "Oh! Our dearest daughter, Midori! You left us so soon. You were so amiable not only to us, but also to every one who came to see us, that we are unable to forget you. The memories of her smile, movement, high-pitched voice and the delicate shades of her psychology revive one by one. Sometimes, I am awakened suddenly at midnight by your call for me heard clearly in a dream. You were all in all to us. Having lost you, we are still now stray sheep. Where does the loneliness come from? You lie down here in the dark cinerarium. Unspeakable sorrow gushes out within our breasts."

Memories and Ideas

"No motion has she now, no force;
    She neither hears nor sees;
Rolled round in earth's diurnal course,
    With rocks, and stones, and trees."   (W. Wordsworth)

"Please, burn incense for the repose of the cinerary urn," said the monk.

The sutra-chanting finished. On both sides of the front of the tombstone, several little chrysanthemums, yellow and white, were solitary and pretty. Below my eyes, in the V-shaped gorge, a few ginkgoes were tinged with brilliant and golden yellow.

Wreathing smoke of incense-sticks swayed to and fro by the light wind. I poured water over the top of the gravestone twice (because Kyoko was absent) which was done to protect it from evils.

Then the monk went away briskly. I was left alone. All of a sudden, I seemed to have heard her voice; "What are you doing? What a poor man papa is! I'm always with you!"

The monk had given me a refreshing feeling. The rising and falling tones of his voice, elegant movements and understandable sutra-chanting brought her to life in my heart momentarily.

It was still before noon. The chilly wind of the late autumn was mixed with the beginning of winter atmosphere. Thin clouds scudded across the sky.

51

第 2 部

A Fairyland

Time passing, I felt elated and took off my coat. In half a dream, I presented my thoughts about John Keats. Images of oncoming words appeared in succession. I completely warmed up to my talk, keeping calm in mind. Recognizing familiar faces one by one, I never felt concerned at all about the audience of more than one hundred, because I had already secured a self-confidently deep understanding of the poet. I had done my very best through nine months since I was asked to give the lecture.

It was in the afternoon of the fourth day in October when I stood on the platform of the Special Hall in No 28 School Building of Meisei University in Hachioji, which stood on the top of woody hill. It was in the midst of autumn.

The title was "Keats's Charm: his Imagination and the Pastoral." I talked about "Endymion" mainly and referred to "Ode to a Nightingale." Without looking at manuscripts, I talked to them quoting several phrases of his letters and lines of his poems. I learned by heart all of them.

During my table talk, however, only one time, I forgot the middle line of his poem, stanza fourth, when emeritus Professor Ms A, the chairman, who was one of my best friends, offered a sheet of paper to me on which "And haply

Memories and Ideas

the Queen moon is on her throne" was written in her own hand. It was a lighting trick. The people seemed not to notice what happened. The hall was in silence. I felt their warm gazes.

Explaining the essence of Keats's imagination in *Endymion* as well as in *Ode to a Nightingale*, I detailed how it was mixed with Pan-Pastoral.

Dian is the queen of Earth, Heaven and Hell in mythology. Endymion seeks for Cynthia in four elements; Earth, Water, fire-Hell and air-Heaven. It symbolizes the growth of a young man's soul. I talked about Endymion overlapping myself. Past and present flashed in my mind's eye, I was John Keats. More and more, my talk heated up.

A storm of hands clapping arose in front of me. In a vision, I felt I had fulfilled my responsibility. Several scholars ran up to me and held out their hands, saying loudly "Bravo!"

I remembered silently the harvest moon of the last night.

第2部

Fairyland Again

Within my Tohoku-Shinkansen's free carriage leaving at 16:51, there were many vacant seats. I was so tired and excited that the quietness brought me self-possession on my way home. I had just finished a lecture titled J. Keats and the fairy in *La Belle Dame sans Merci*, one hour ago at the Fairy Museum in Utsunomiya.

It was two o'clock in the afternoon of the 22nd day in June when I stood on the platform at the conference room in the Museum, which stood at the foot of Futara-san shrine. It was one day after the summer solstice on which many fairies appeared in *A Midsummer Night's Dream* of Shakespeare.

I was calm in mind and full of confidence because I got a preview of the room. I prepared for the speech for more than five months. I learned by heart the ballad, word by word, completely. In my own words, I was able to talk about its deep meaning correlating it with Keats' *Ode on Melancholy*, with several parts in his letters; "O for a Life of Sensation rather than of Thought!"

Many in the audience seemed to be highly-educated. I placed the focus on "the elfin grot" which was a symbol of women. At the same time, it means *anima* of Carl G. Jung (1875–1961); the collective unconsciousness of men.

54

Memories and Ideas

Explaining the essence of Keats' imagination, which belongs
to intellectual empathy, I talked about the significant relation
between the knight and the fairy, overlapping with myself
when I was young. Past and present flashed in my mind's
eye, momentarily. I was the knight in the Arthurian legends.
More and more my talk heated up.

> She took me to her elfin grot,
>   And there she wept and sigh'd full sore;
> And there I shut her wild, wild eyes
>   With kisses four.   (29–31)

Why "she wept"? Why "she sigh'd full sore"? Between the
first line and the second line, we guess something happened
to them. The ballad does not say anything. We may only
guess. There is the essence of the ballad.

Before marriage, men may have the chance to meet la
Bell Dame sans Merci. The less mercy she has, the more
memorable she will become to them.

Time passing, I felt elated and took off my coat. Half
dreaming, I presented my meditation about the knight who
was Keats. Images of coming words appeared in succession.
I completely warmed to my talk.

He had a lover named Fanny Brawne, who was eighteen
years old. She liked dancing. He was "alone and palely
loitering" in his imagination.

第 2 部

An Optimistic Driver

"Ah! Sorry, sir, I have completely forgotten to put up the flag on the taxi meter. I was too much occupied with talking," said the driver with an awkward smile, when I asked him, "How much?"

With his curly hair and short-beard, both comfortably suited, he looked like someone who would find a lot of fun in life. He seemed to have a host of entertaining stories, and a flair for telling them.

"I just came to Oita, last year," said he nonchalantly. "Here fish is fresh, air clean and people kind. Everything is OK. It is quite different from Tokyo."

"My wife was born in Oita. I was born and grew up in Nerima Ward in Tokyo. But Tokyo is nowadays becoming worse and worse," he continued to speak at a breath.

"With my wife's advice, I left Tokyo, my native place, and moved over here to live in Oita, which is near Beppu, the famous hot spring city, where I always enjoy myself, when I am off duty. Yes, for me this place is a sort of paradise, sir."

His impulse for talking seemed uncontrollable. "I'm fond of Noh farces, films and the kabuki. I'm now sixty-five years old. Without failing to catch an opportunity of retirement from the commercial company in Tokyo, I determined to

Memories and Ideas

cross the Rubicon. I have enjoyed my life up till now. Oita was for me an unknown land. But I'm very happy now, thanks to my wife," it was as if he were under the genial influence of his own magic words.

It was the afternoon of the twenty-first day of September, the autumn equinox, when we went to my native land and offered a bunch of flowers at my ancestral grave. It is the small, quiet, inconvenient village of Kami-Hetsugi, fourteen kilometers away from the city of Oita. We visited several relations.

After the short stay of busy hours, we had to call a taxi again to go to the nearest railway station. The driver was a native and also a talkative person as pleasant as the driver we had met in Oita City. Knowing that I was born and brought up here and now living in Tokyo, he seemed to have felt familiar with me. He began to reply to my casual questions.

"Why don't you return to this nice village? Nowhere is more peaceful and safer than here in the world," said he, gazing at me.

I know it. But I have many complex reasons to want to live in Tokyo.

Getting off from the taxi, we paid him enough.

第 2 部

To Bury the Hair and Nail in our Ancestral Graveyard

It was in the early morning on the twenty-fourth day of July when I came to the entrance of our ancestral grave at Kami-Hetugi in Oita. It stands halfway up Turugajyo Hill, one hundred meters above sea level, where there was an historical battle in the seventeenth century.

My village is nestling under the hill.

There seemed no sign of people moving outdoors. Feeling a bit of sultry summer in the warm winds, I trudged up the mountain path with a knapsack on my back.

Step by step, the past came again dimly as well as vividly. In the small village, where lived one hundred and fifty people, I was obliged to face up to myself in the twenties. On the way to the grave, the house in which I had passed long melancholy days stood as it was.

The grave was absolutely in silence. I heard songs of a bush warbler in flight. I swept devotedly around the tomb with a besom that I had made on the spot with the twigs of *sakaki* (which was known as a sacred tree). Working gloves became dirty very soon. Surrounded by oaks, pine-trees and deciduous trees, the graveyard was wild in rotten fallen leaves.

Memories and Ideas

Offering a piece of mountain lily, I burned incense. Wreathing smoke of incense-sticks swayed to and fro in the dim wind. Chanting sutra phrases, I watered the top of the tombstone several times to protect it from the severe heat in daytime. It was my apology for a long absence.

After taking a rest, I began to dig the earth with the favorite shovel which I had brought with me. The soil was rather hard. Earthworms were still sleepy. I made a little hole about twenty centimeters wide and fifteen centimeters deep. Into it, I put with a prayer my hair and nails which had been enveloped with the old *Oita Godo-Shinbun* paper. For two years, I had prepared, keeping the hair and nails, for this day.

Slowly, I covered them with the earth. The dead were once buried as they naturally were. Thinking how and when the dead were buried, the soil becomes spiritual. My unknown grandparents have slept here, together with my parents, two elder brothers and a younger sister. The native place as well as the ancestral grave is holy, beyond imagination.

The older I become, the more I long for the native place in which I battled with myself desperately.

Then I felt as if someone was approaching.

第 2 部

Nine Minutes

"It is a great honor for me to have you as my cataract doctor," I said bowing deeply to Dr. Inoue, who was known as one of the most skillful eye doctors in our country.

With no letter of introduction, patients are not always able to choose their doctors in a hospital.

Relying completely on him, I climbed up, in silence, to the inclined operating chair, with my head wrapped in vinyl hair cap and my bust covered with short vinyl gown.

He seemed to have given a local anesthesia to my right eye. The operation had begun. For a little while, I had a sort of stimulation in my shoulders, arms, legs and the whole body. Soon it was gone. I felt that the laser beams burned the turbidity of the crystalline lens little by little. I also recognized clearly the process of operation moment by moment. In my right eye, delicate wine-colored and light-blue colored flames were burning mixed together and flickering to and fro.

Gradually, there seemed to appear a black hole or a microcosmic space. I could not believe this kind of spectacle. The black hole enlarged as the burning of laser beams proceeded. At that time when the turbidity of the eye lens had gone, a little golden globe like a fairy cup appeared. I knew in my imagination it was an artificial lens. In a moment,

60

Memories and Ideas

I was seeing a space exploration in the eye. Without being conscious of it, the operation became a sort of pleasure which I had never felt.

"Oh, a wonderful scene I have now in my eye. How I am enjoying the four-dimensional world," I said loudly with a little excitement.

No sooner the little elfin globe or cup settled down into the black hole than he told me that the operation had finished. I was still in the midst of a dream. I wanted the fairy tale in my eye to continue longer.

"Return to the room, please. Everything is OK," he said again smiling.

On my way to the room with a veteran nurse, passing through patients waiting for their conducts with worried airs, I was told by her that it had taken only nine minutes to perform the operation. Because of his skillful practice, a lot of patients come up to his hospital from many parts of Japan. I noticed the cataract operation took more than fifteen minutes.

"We have never heard such a pleasurable chatter as you did while the doctor was performing the operation," she said beamingly.

61

第 2 部

A Couple of my Front Teeth

"Now, I will give your front teeth's gums a local anesthetic," our family dentist, Dr. Kohda said to me clearly.

"Is it serious?" I asked him, expecting a good reply.

"It is not always good, but I will try," said he determinedly.

Since two days before, a couple of my upper front teeth had begun to ache.

The gums had swollen. Only a couple of my upper front teeth were left. They had become fragile at the roots according to an X-ray examination. They barely supported the whole upper artificial teeth. It was a symbol of my age. However, I wanted to chew tasty foods with my own teeth, as long as possible, even if it might be hard a little.

"I owe to you that I have still more than sixteen teeth," I said to him, with gratitude.

He smiled with warm sympathy.

The next moment, I felt pain and my palate paralyzed when I salivated a little, bitterly.

He had put a small medical knife on the suppurating part without saying a word. I listened to awkward sounds of shaving the tooth, the operation of which continued intermittently, which got on my nerves. I felt bitter saliva flow out little by little inside my mouth. The strange taste made me feel nausea. It was too unpleasant for words.

Several minutes passed in silence except for the sounds of medical implements touching each other.

"Wash your mouth, please," said he, calmly.

An inexpressible taste remained, yet. I was irritated and the ticking time was reluctant.

Suddenly, I dreamed and the vision of a roasted chicken passed by. It was slowly cooked for three hours, spreading olive and garlic enough on it. It was gradually done to beautiful golden brown, scorched here and there smelling very delicious. The fragrance of the meat and chicken with blackened spotted granular stimulated my appetite.

In a moment I lost myself.

I gargled repeatedly. Blood died away unwillingly.

I felt my aging terribly. Year after year, not only every organ in my palate, but also other parts in my whole body have become worse in their functions.

"This time it's OK. You had better not take coffee for an hour. Come again, in two days, please," said he disinterestedly.

On my way home, I asked myself.

'What is my Idealism?"

第2部

My Friend, Dr. Furukawa

"You are a person rather hard to get on with." My friend Dr. Furukawa abruptly said to me. It was in our annual class meeting, when I heard the ironical remarks.

He was our home doctor and one of my closest and most trustworthy friends. We were old playmates in the days of Oita Middle School students. So I couldn't believe his words at that moment.

Returning home, I told the event to my wife Kyoko, who laughed a little, saying, "Oh, yes, he is right. You are a person sometimes difficult to understand."

Deeply shocked, but secretly worrying, that night I could not sleep well.

Several months later, Dr Furukawa, his wife Mineko-san and both of us dined together in the room named Zangetsu (the moon at dawn) of Chinzan-so, in Bunkyo-ku, Tokyo. The atmosphere was nice. The room was in a solitary, small cottage, an annex located within the garden about sixty meters away from the main building. It was pure Japanese-style cottage, a sort of tea arbor. We had long kept a friendly relation-ship including all our family members. This time we invited them in celebration of his retirement from Chief Director of the Maruyama Sogo Hosipital, Saitama City.

We dined, drank and at the climax in our chattering, I asked him, "Do you remember your words that Mr. Takahashi is a person hard to get on with?" With warm smile on the lips, instantly he said. "No, I don't." Mineko-san was silent, perhaps sensitively. Kyoko was eating eagerly, saying nothing. But they were full of affectionate breathings. From the wide Japanese-style shoji-windows, the crescent was casting its slight beams into Zangetsu-room. A revelation flashed upon my inward eye, which came from our mutual confidence. If my friend's tongue should ever slip, time would not fail to veil it cordially. There was a deeply blessed moment. However, heartily I reflected on my own doings before and tasted his frank words.

He passed away three months ago, on the very first day of this year. Since then, I cannot recover myself from a strange state of depression. His friendship has taken root deep inside my soul. His dead face was so divinely beautiful that I could not help thinking the noble features of Buddha. He had donated his blood more than two hundred times in his lifetime. A man dies as he lived.

I feel shame about myself. I have lived making troubles for many people. "You are a person hard to get on with." "You have your own way." His simple words helped me understand what I really was and what I had really never wanted to disclose.

Anyway, I want to live as I am. I don't know any other way. I cannot live without something like a hope. I want to have one more book written by my vivid inward voice.

第2部

Aging is an Unknown Journey

Aging is an unknown journey. Nobody knows the desti-
nation or the process of its expedition.

With a decline of organic functions of my body, I am ill at
ease. Something has changed in my brain, mind and heart.
Movements of my body do not obey my will. Weird shadows
in my consciousness are increasing. I miss my footing on the
stairs when I am unable to raise accurately my feet higher
than the height of the steps. Moreover, in daytime I saunter
in the house here and there aimlessly.

My MRI shows my brain has greatly shrunk. Brain cells
seem to have much decreased. I am troubled with buzzing in
the ears, giddiness, poor memory, mishearing and enigmatic
ideas which appear or disappear in my mind; these are my
routine evil friends now that I am 88 years old.

Making my tongue move active-slowly within my mouth,
I am horrified to feel the gap between a few remained teeth
widened, together with the shrinkage of the cartilage in
the mouth. Only a couple of my upper front teeth are left.
They have become fragile at the roots according to an X-ray
examination. I have become of weak sight as well as dull
smell. I often forget that the kettle is boiling.

These negative conditions of the faculty of sensation make

other functions of my body shrivel. Unconsciously, I cough and have much phlegm thin or tough. My eyes shed tears and lips drop saliva.

"Yushiro-san, you walk with a heavy stoop. Be careful," Kyoko advises me.

She is an air-like trainer for me. She encourages me. I thank her much for her warm care. In nearby Odakyu OX, I see men of my generation who keep their heads always down. In many cases, they seem to live by themselves.

I walk lonely with my tiptoes up, every early evening for half an hour around the house, remembering various things; I am sinful. I injured many people's minds and hearts, particularly my wife, Kyoko, all unconsciously.

However, I am sure the fine carriage is most important, when we are old. I walk keeping the chin down, looking straight on. It leads to my way of life; I want to live creatively and proudly through my life. The past is the past. Death is to be "a consummation devoutly to be wished." (Shakespeare).

Considering these depressive things, I do not like going out of doors after sunset when I am deprived of the sense of direction. Mysterious darkness in my mind and body widens its territory rapidly.

II

Seasons, Trees and Worms

第 2 部

The Rain in the Season for Leaf-buds to Grow

Silent sounds of the rain, I heard them dreamily. I slept a sleep that knew no dawn. How nice the early spring is! I enjoyed the dream without dream between sleeping and waking. It was a half-real world in which I was.

This year we had a particularly severe cold. Winter leaves hesitatingly. Spring is now just around the corner. I have a golden time to appreciate the weather when the season of rain for leaf-buds to grow has begun.

In our garden, a maple tree, which is deciduous, has no leaf yet. It is still naked. It stands in its own meditation. There is no vanity in it. Well, I'm turning myself into the maple tree because I have nothing to do with any superficiality in the world. We cannot deceive the past, as the naked trees cannot. There is no lie with them. They stand in their truth.

In spring and summer, plants have life force inside. As the days become shorter and the thermometer falls, they cease to produce this life-giving pigment. In later autumn, the leaves shift the phase. As chlorophyll breaks down, other pigments and their colors, those that put mask before by presence of chlorophyll, appear. It is the oranges, reds and purples of carotene and anthocyanin that are revealed. Day

Memories and Ideas

by day, many plants begin to be naked.

All living things are to pass away. But plants rise from death yearly. In the midst of winter, they fight for a new life under the earth. Avoiding wastefulness, they keep life force. Their black-naked figures signify death as well as life itself.

The rain of leaf-buds in early spring is nothing but the blessing of God. It gives me the pleasure of life. At dawn on the tenth day of March, hearing the impressive sounds of rain dreamily, all of a sudden, I recalled a stanza in *The Daffodils* of Wordsworth.

"They flash upon that inward eye
Which is the bliss of solitude;
And then my heart with pleasure fills,
And dances with the daffodils."

Memories of the past flashed upon my heart. The silent melody of the rain lingered a while everywhere.

At the same time, I felt that the loveliness of young maple leaves and the freshness of persimmon leaves were coming out very soon. The beauty of a season is as short as the beauty of juvenility.

第 2 部

The Persimmon Tree in Early Spring

Through the curtain, I look at the garden absent-mindedly, off and on, when I get tired of reading and writing. Our persimmon stands unshapely with its curved trunks and twisted branches. The skyline, which its branches and twigs produce, is like an unfolded umbrella with ribs only and no panels.

I remember the gardener K saying that the tree has endured so many injuries. He added that there were few people who could trim persimmons in the neighborhood.

Trimming of any garden tree makes an old man comfortable. When I am depressed, the tree stimulates me.

"Hello! How are you? Don't worry. Live in the present."

When I hear the encouraging words, it reminds me of W. Pater's "The Renaissance," He also says "observe things as they are."

The tree has grown with us honestly. While it was young, it often made a fool of strong typhoons. We exerted our ingenuity to prevent the trunks being broken down, tightening them with strings and poles. To be strange, at the root, the trunk divided itself into three. The wind used to make the trunks bend violently. Their struggle against heavy winds brought them several knots, which let them lose their normal colors, turning black. The awkwardness grieves in early

Memories and Ideas

spring. However, its shape as it is, relaxes my mind.

The deciduous tree seems solitary, particularly on moonlit nights. The black naked figure tells me truth and thoughts in the world. There is no show about it. It seems to be proud of itself.

Under the tree, there are various forms of life; earthworms, moles, green caterpillars, ants, unknown little worms—they are now active a little—which foster microscopic organisms.

Thanks to the fertile ground, which we made, every year we have enjoyed its fruits. Nature recycles, bringing me hopes.

Some of its fruits tasted half sour at first, while others were sweet. But year by year, all of them became delicious, as Kyoko grew gradually docile to me.

Spring is near at hand. After we cut twigs as well as branches, heads and sides of them began to have germs. Their naked figures will take fresh dress tomorrow, and smell softly. I imagine the slight sounds of the sap running within the trunks. I hear life murmur, or see it glisten in my mind's eye.

The tree is my significant friend, it gives me a vital force.

"Yushiro! Never give up until you finish publishing two more books," it says, with a smile.

A new moon has appeared dimly among the branches. The evening wind is cold yet.

第 2 部

Little Creatures in the Soil

Opening the barn door silently, I took out my favorite small shovel. I began to weed out the garden. The thriving weeds had called me out.

In a moment, swarms of gnats and little mosquitoes attacked me, buzzing. I equipped myself for laboring with a long sleeve-shirt and a pair of rough trousers as well as workman's split-toed heavy-cloth shoes, army-gloves, sunglasses, and I tied a towel around my head.

The air was soft with a breath of wind; the early morning light gleamed freshly as white clouds disappeared in the sky. Somewhat warm air brought the delightful summer scent. It contained a hint of sweet flowers, a pinch of perennial saururaceae plants and the lush loamy smell of rich soil damped with yesterday's rain.

Under the persimmon tree occupying the area of one-third of our garden, where various grasses are mixed with Japanese gingers, I used to find dead bodies of little creatures and cicadas. They would probably lure out nocturnal detritus feeders, slugs, snails, earthworms and bugs. These slow moving members of graveyard worm, detritivores, are among the invertebrates. As natural creatures, we humans owe much to them. Each insect provides a small window

74

Memories and Ideas

into a whole web of life-cycles within the earth of which I am miserably ignorant.

Hiding themselves by the trunk of a persimmon tree, or inside the soil, or among the-plucked weeds piled at the root of the tree, they are silent. Earthworms have fine bristles and chaetae, on each of their body segments. It is the friction between these and the ground that allows them to creep slowly and burrow into the soil so easily. Gastropods like snails and slugs have tentacles with which they sample their environment, sensing light and dark, flavors and odors. Their being itself makes our unknown world fertile. They are my friends to whom I talk.

"How are you? I am very happy to meet you again,"

"You are our unconsciousness, aren't you?" I said to them with the hearty reverence.

They belong to the collective unconsciousness of Carl G. Jung (1875–1961). They make a rhythm of Nature having vibration, wavelength, silence, and unlimited possibility which add an active emotion to our spiritual-daily life; it requires me to sleep well, to get up early in the morning, to take exercises regularly, to read books, to chew foods well, to write something constantly. Thanks to their holy divinity; I can live on hoping for the best.

But usually I have no sooner caught sight of them than I hesitate and retreat from them a little.

"See you again," I am apt to say in secret to them.

第 2 部

A Whiff of Fresh Air

"I'm sure, the earth has got angry, greatly," I said to Kyoko.

"I can no more bear the abnormal climate, I am on the point of losing my mental and spiritual balance," she chimed in.

Through the curtain, I can see deep white summer clouds floating in the sky. Cicadas sing all around. On persimmon leaves in our garden, I can see shadows clearly. In spite of the terrible heat, autumn is near at hand; today is the tenth day of August.

"Please, take it easy, Yushiro-san," she said to me.

It passed five o'clock in the afternoon. Under the big green tree, the soil was discolored brown. Cast-off shells of cicadas and dried earthworms could be found everywhere. On the backs of half-decayed fallen leaves, circular-gray-colored little worms were moving here and there. Such slow-moving insects of the dark-wet ground are able to bear the severe heat.

Turning on the tap at the garden corner, I trained the hose on the scorched and cracked ground. The physical work is not only one of my duties every evening, and it refreshes me. I feel that weeds, insects, trees and brown-colored earth whisper to me to bring them water quickly.

Memories and Ideas

Many leaves of the persimmon made themselves round into the shape of rugby balls due to the heat. The spray falls forcibly on the sad-miserable leaves and revives them in a moment. No sooner had water begun to flow out, than they seemed to become vivid again. I felt my right thumb benumbed a little. Dust rose from the earth, lightly. It attacked itself to my whole body. The touch of spouting water through the hose reminds me of my young days. The lower half of my trousers and long sleeves of my shirt are wet to the skin. Water flies away from me five meters away. Mosquitoes come upon me all at once.

While I repeat watering the corners several times, stuffy hot air here and there in our garden gradually disperses. Cicadas have begun to sing more loudly.

Little birds come to twigs of the tree on which they are a-tilt in their heads and watch for earth insects.

There were widened mackerel clouds in the sky and the wind had been softened a little.

第 2 部

The *Kinmokusei* in our Garden

"How nice they are! From the *kinmokusei* comes to us a faint but nice aroma. Autumn is now with us, Yushiro-san," Kyoko said, more than half to herself.

"Are they really? At last we are able to recover ourselves. Anyway, we had a long severe heat wave, over 36 degrees C. in summer," I responded to her.

In this season, we have the *kinmokusei*, a variety of fragrant olives native to Asia, wherever we may go in the suburbs of Tokyo. The tree seems, almost through the year, to be a blob-shaped arboreal nonentity. One day in fall, suddenly, she is transformed, though her coming-out figure is not as effective as that of the cherry blossom in spring.

Today is the 28th day in September and the *kinmokusei* in our garden has bloomed all at once. Every year, the date almost never changes. It is surprising to know how mysterious Nature's significant dispensation is.

The *kinmokusei* shows us her tiny golden fruit-flowers like secret meetings of fairies which are the spirits in the tree. At their gathering place between slender but not very nice leaves, they are so modest that no one but smell-sensitive people would pay any attention to them, though they have filled the whole tree by making tiny groups in about twenty-

78

five fruit-flowers. Their keen smell carries me to the unknown old days where human beings lived as if they were wild animals.

This dull light-brown tree comes alive only a few days in a year. As the flowers are fragile, even a slight rain turns them terribly miserable. After scattering tiny fruit-flowers here and there, however, the fragrance remains around for a little while. The smell is mellow and scented when everything else is winding down, withdrawing, withering or, besides, tending toward darkness and decay. The keen-sweet atmosphere which they give forth is the sensual core of October in our country.

The *kinmokusei* is against the grain of the season's conventional idea of melancholy. Her golden-sweet aromas charm our senses of vision and smell. It gives me a selective indulgence as well as an exercise in concentration. Her attractive smell is as unrestrained as anything wafted to our eyes and nose in the wake of a wild and elegant lady we happen to pass by in a street.

I like the unpretentious *kinmokusei* in the brief moment in the autumnal sunlight. It seems an example necessary for me; the older a person is, the more reserved he becomes. Leaving an impressive aftereffect one week later, it makes me feel a sort of pleasure at the possibilities hidden in humble or unexpected things. Autumn does not always mean sadness in the transience of everything.

第 2 部

Fallen Leaves

A little bird was turning fallen leaves searching for insects to feed upon in our garden. Looking at it through the curtain of the study, my heart leaped up. Suddenly, I wanted to participate in its movement.

I was brimful of vigor. Last night, I slept well. There was not a speck of cloud in the sky. It was rather warm for the morning of the second day of November.

Under the persimmon tree, there was a carpet of fallen leaves. The bird had left, but the sign of its little breathing sounds remained. They were tinged with yellow, red, dark brown and delicate liver colors. Moreover, here and there, I was able to see crushed mellowed persimmon fruits. Little insects were flying around them.

Nostalgic smells of the earth, fallen leaves, fruits and the pretty bird intoxicated my heart deep to it's core in a moment.

However, fallen leaves scatter around on windy days. I have a custom to gather and bury them in the 40 x 30 cm hole which I dug before. Silent symphony of autumn smells was gorgeous. Feeling it with my mind's ear, I gardened for a while.

It rained two days ago. The backs of fallen leaves were wet. I found some water. Under them, many perennial plants of the family saururaceae and lichens were encroaching aggressively everywhere to the persimmon trunk.

Earthworms are my friends. Each insect provides a small window into a whole fabric of life circles within the ground of which we know almost nothing.

The soil was soft. Before long, I noticed there were droppings of cats and dogs, or shed-skins of cicadas. They would perhaps lure out detritus feeders that love darkness. These slow-moving worms of the dark-wet ground are known as detritivores, and some invertebrates to which we humans should be most grateful.

Everything natural that falls, or is dropped or buried, whether plants, from flowers and fruits to leaves and twigs, or animals from shed-skin, fur and feces to whole carcasses—somehow disappears, without our noticing, thanks to nature's recycling system performed by the nocturnal creatures.

I buried fallen leaves in the hole and trod on them firmly. Within a month, they sweat and resolve into its original elements. Our soil becomes fertile. I have done this for more than forty years.

Golden leaves that once surrounded ripe fruits, flutter down silently now and then, by the slight wind, in my regretful glance. I realize what it is to live and to die. They are "like the things of man," and "it is the bright man born for." (Hopkins)

I stretched myself and breathed deeply when several sparrows flew down.

III
Wife and Husband

第 2 部

Communication between Kyoko and I

"Yushiro-san, I will go to Nakajima chiropractic Clinic in Chofu," Kyoko said to me weakly.

"Take it easy, please," said I.

"No, you had better ask 'what is the matter with you?' in this case, and I want your kind words," she complained.

"Thinking of John Keats, you are indifferent to me, whenever I may say something to you. You deviate from other people in the world," said she ironically.

She is right. I am an absent-minded man, and egoistic in everything. In my mind, daily things did not exist at all till recent days. But I have gradually understood that the considerate communication with Kyoko was very important.

She is always beside me; she cooks, washes and cares for me in detail. In spite of it, I have felt she was the air and the water. I could breathe and drink freely whatever I might want. It was natural for me to take it for granted that she would do as I wanted.

Recently, some of my friends who lost their wives are obliged to live at care-houses for old people. They are unwilling to reply to a letter I write to them. I feel deep sadness to imagine how they are solitary and miserable.

84

Janus runs after me minute by minute, with a big scythe in his hand. The older I am, the more mutual sympathy I have to keep on even in our routine conversation.

The convenience with which I am able to work comfortably everyday at the age of eighty-eight, owes to her wise faithfulness. I have no words to say in excuse to her.

"Take care, please, Kyoko," I said, following her to the entrance hall.

Scarcely had I remorse in my mind before she disappeared. By nature, she is weak in the stomach. Whenever something unpleasant may happen, spiritual contradiction, which is hidden within the unconsciousness, concentrates on the weakest spot of the body. As for her, it is the stomach.

She excels in the five senses. Particularly, she is pre-eminent above the rest for her keen nose and hearing which contribute to her nice cooking. Moreover, she is able to guess the atmosphere of circumstances, sensitively.

I think it seems better to choose words when we talk. A careless slip of my tongue injures her unbelievably. If she should be sick in bed, what shall I do? The idealism of mine has no use in emergency. Well, I will be silent whenever I notice any delicate change in the movement of her pupils and mouth.

第 2 部

A Bottle of Sake and Youth

"Yushiro! You seem to consist of sake. Recently, you drink it every night. You used to drink only three times a week, a couple of years ago, didn't you?" said Kyoko softly.

"Yes, so it was! I have been under a great stress these days. Everything is against me, and I'm aging rapidly. So I drink, no, I cannot help drinking. But just one small bottle of sake with ices, which is rather healthy," I emphasized.

"That's OK, You cook by yourself even as a side dish something like *nuta*. I can expect nothing better for you," she spoke highly of me, with a smile.

"I'm now a miserable martyr to a heavy backache. While I sip sake little by little in the evening, tasting the self-cooked *nuta*, I forget my troubles. Youth returns to me vaguely in a moment."

"Ah! for the change 'twixt. Now and Then!
This breathing house not built with hand,
This body that does me grievous wrong,
O'er aery cliffs and glittering sands,
How lightly then it flash'd along—"   (S. T. Coleridge)

I remember I was not used to becoming tired, over anything I might do. I did everything without hesitation. In travelling, I did not care about the weather. But now I'm very cautious in doing anything.

"I'm sure, you are healthy because of your prudent way of living not only in drinking, but in doing everything else," she said with a warm but ironical smile.

Her character is quite the opposite of mine. She is active and bold in her way of living. She is always a strict, realistic and gentle adviser for me as well as a critic.

"Yushiro! You are not so old. The vesper-bell of your youth has not yet tolled. Because youth is a bold masker and it only puts on strange disguise to make believe that it is gone. You live even now with youth. Youth is your house- mate still," she soothed me.

Her tolerance and encouraging words are a slight diversion for me, who am full of contradictions, capricious, shilly-shally and mushy. She always lifts my spirits, when I am in distress.

Youth may be only a fond conceit, as long as a man keeps up his own little hope or an ideal in his mind. And he seems to be fresh in body, and in mind.

第 2 部

Our Vegetable Soup

"Please tell me how to make our great soup?" I asked Kyoko.

"It is nice of you," putting out a feeler, she said with a smile. It was in the early evening of January eleventh when I begged her to tell me the recipe. Aging demands me to be independent. I don't know how to do when I will be alone.

"At first, prepare all the ingredients that are primarily necessary. You should have a middle-sized onion and a potato, several pieces of pumpkin, a little bit of carrot, one spoonful of butter, a cup of milk and one piece of bouillon," she continued.

"The problem is whether you put away the pumpkin's peels or not. They give dark colors to the soup and the appearance is fatally important," she said.

"Next, prepare a pot. Cut the potato and onion into little dices, and pour about 200cc water into the pot until it soaks the ingredients, and then simmer them gently with a low heat in the pot with the lid on. When they begin to boil, put one piece of bouillon and grated carrot a little into the pot. You had better boil them down to a pulp-condition for a while, since making a soup means to draw out foodstuff's extracts by heating them."

Memories and Ideas

"Remember, Yushiro-san, a bit of salt, pepper and butter. They are conclusive factors with which to flavor the soup," she said, gazing at me.

I emptied the mixed vegetable juice as well as 100 cc plus alpha quantity of milk into the mixer for my own share.

I switched it on for one minute.

The sound which the simple machine makes let my stimulation release.

That was OK, I thought.

Scarcely had I sipped it a little when inexplicable deep-soft deliciousness let the saliva ooze out with joyfulness.

"Wow, how tasty this is!" I said loudly.

"The moment we taste the good soup, we feel as if the stiffness in our shoulders is suddenly gone. We don't know why such sensation occurs. We find our soup stocks present us with the easiest way to get nutrition," said Kyoko proudly.

That is her philosophy of our family soup.

Recently I have been influenced by her idea. Eating is the biggest pleasure in life. It is the high light in daily life. Particularly, soup is important. It can be served at the very beginning of the meal, and it may leave a long-lasting impression throughout the following courses.

"I have never thought that I can appreciate Yushiro-san's soup at our dinner, while I have become seventy-five years old," Kyoko said pleasantly.

第2部

Homemade Orange Marmalade Jam

"How nice this jam is!" tasting it a little, I said loudly.

"Is it really? I'm very happy to hear that. Last night, late, I added to it, as a secret flavor, a little of the best brandy," Kyoko said, smiling.

It was about eight o'clock in the morning of the sixth day of January when I tasted, for the first time, our homemade orange marmalade jam.

At the end of December, one of my relations, Ms Iwamoto who lives in Beppu, near Oita, sent us several oranges that grew in her garden. Beppu is famous for hot springs and beautiful scenery with the seaside and mountains. The climate is mild. Oranges are delicious.

It is precious for us in Tokyo to have oranges grown without agricultural chemicals. We planned to make jam from them.

These are the necessary ingredients; several orange peels sliced down to pieces, one small bottle of honey, 180 ml bottle of white wine and 360 ml bottle of water.

I took two tangerines and carefully pared them, the orange peels hanging in irregular strips over the large but sharp knife. I put the peels on a longer board and cut them into small pieces. Placing the cool and bright-yellow peels in a

Memories and Ideas

clear medium sized bowl, I measured out one-hundred-and-eighty ml of fragrant white wine and three-hundred-and-sixty ml of water. After that, I tossed the empty pet bottle in the trash and it bounced into the hole with a thud.

The first day, we mixed and boiled the peel in a casserole for three hours. In the end, she added, as a secret ingredient, one piece of lemon peel and a large spoonful of lemon juice. We let it sit one night. On the second day, we continued stewing it for three more hours. I noticed that the color deepened. On the third day, we used a mixer for a few minutes. After that, we boiled them again for two hours.

"I think it is better to have some pieces of peel left in shape as they are."

She agreed with me.

In the process of making the jam, I sometimes tried to taste it. It was a sort of childish, nostalgic and thrillingly delicate experience. We devoted ourselves carefully to making jam over three days. But I did not know what she did, in secret, at the end of the third day.

One of my pleasures is; getting up early, I take three pieces of cracker with home-made jam, a cup of coffee and two pieces of seasonal fruits. When I open the door of the refrigerator to take out a jam pot, I feel the rich and golden scent hanging in the air. In the morning twilight, the faint and delicious flavour, the mellow brown color, the solitary silence and my healthy four score years and eight—these things give me, in a moment, a drunken feeling.

第 2 部

March Cold in my Mind

The local Odakyu Line train arrived at Komae Station. The platform was exposed to the chilly wind. The shadow of March evening was thickening into night. I was on the way home from a meeting in Shinjuku.

I felt uneasy all of a sudden. Unfortunately, there was no taxi at the cab stand. I was obliged to wait ten minutes. I like to walk back to my house, usually.

A taxi came. I knew the driver by sight. I had no sooner fallen into a slumber than the taxi reached my house.

"It's funny, I feel slightly like vomiting, Kyoko!" said I.

"You had better go to bed as soon as possible! Be careful. March weather is extremely capricious and it has become cold this evening," said she.

Without taking a bath, with no dinner and only taking my favorite medicine, I went to bed.

I was troubled by a nightmare. It seemed in the later night that I suddenly realized I hadn't relieved myself since this morning. I had a violent purging and repeated evacuations of the bowels. I felt a pain in the intestines.

How many hours passed I did not know. After several deep sleep waves, I was conscious of a vague line of light around me. It seemed either at dawn or at midnight. I was in an old

Memories and Ideas

warm dream.

"Mind your steps, Sensei!" a considerate lady said to me when she led me to the handrail in Shinjuku Station's downward stairs. She is one of our meeting members.

"When you decide to live in a Care House, I will visit you monthly and listen to your lecture, Sensei!" one of them said loudly when we parted. They had been my students years before. They now have outgrown their charms, except in my own eyes.

While talking with them, sometimes I have an illusion that I am an Oberon surrounded by elegant fairies.

Suddenly, I felt an angel touch on my forehead. It smelt like the personal scent of Kyoko's hand.

"You said something in delirium, but looked happy, Yushiro-san!" She said with a smile.

"Take water, a little, and you will have a better sleep," she continued and put the blanket to rights.

It had begun to rain.

第2部

June is near at Hand

"Oh! It's very nice. Thank you very much for your thoughtfulness," I said to Kyoko.

There lay on the table several boiled beans, cut tomatoes and onions in round slices, fried potato crisps and hashed cucumbers seasoned with vinegar. Through the year, she gets fresh vegetables from the nearby farmer's stand. Seasonal vegetables are my capital accompaniments to sake.

"I envy you! I wish I could drink either wine or sake a little," she said regretfully.

Her constitution does not suit any alcohol.

The moonlight, stealing in from the window, blends with the light of the evening. Sipping sake, I think back.

Light exercises in the early evening and a cup of sake are exquisite. Refreshing fatigue after reading and writing calls for alcohol a little. Particularly June is the best season when weeds grow thick in our garden. I like to cut the rampant weeds by breaking the ground. I use a favorite hoe which I got forty years ago. I feel a vital force through earthly work.

"Every clod feels a stir of might,
    An instinct within it that reaches and towers
And, grouping blindly above it for light,

Memories and Ideas

Climbs to a soul in grass and flowers;"

(Lowell, "June")

I love our garden, because we have enriched the soil by burying kitchen waste for more than forty years. Luxuriant weeds seem to have something to whisper to us every day.

"You enjoy solitude with sake, looking absent-mindedly at persimmons, your inside life might be gorgeous, isn't it?" She said.

She understands me deeply. I taste sake with dishes to my core.

Mid-summer's Day, which is the herald of June, is near at hand. The flush of life is full in our garden. Every clod broken by the hoe is black and fresh. Within it sometimes lies a little earthworm. Underground is another world as well as a domain of an unconsciousness where spirits live. I do not know what they are. A drop of sake brings me spirit in the brink of an eyelid like fairy. Little birds sit on green branches of the persimmon in the early evening sun and are a-tilt like blossoms among the leaves. The buttercup catches the soft beams in its chalice.

"Eggplants are ripe enough for eating and turnips also are seasonal, tomorrow I will have them for you," she said to me, with a smile.

95

第 2 部

Ireland, a Vision

"I fractured the third toe of my left foot when I knelt down a while ago. Ah! I am awfully sorry, Yushiro!" Kyoko told me half sobbing.

It was in the afternoon of the thirteenth day of May, when I heard of her accident, soon after my returning from the poetry reading in Shinjuku. Three days later, we were to start for Ireland to celebrate our fortieth anniversary.

Everything was ready, even with the corset as a talisman in case of backache, I had packed in my baggage.

"What did you say?" I immediately asked her.

An awkward silence hung between us for a few seconds. Kyoko, looking pale in an abstracted state of mind, her head drooping and tears shinning dimly on her eyes.

Twelve years ago, while I was in Cambridge as a visiting fellow to Darwin College, Kyoko and I enjoyed Sligo in Ireland for one week. It was her first visit. I never forget how she appreciated Guinness, original Irish beer, and enjoyed its ancient mythologies and fairy tales.

I belong to the Yeats's Society in Japan for a long while. This time, too, I intended to guide her through Ireland as much as possible.

Memories and Ideas

We love the atmosphere in the Irish pub. The Irish people are easy to approach and talk to, particularly in the pubs. In Sligo, which is in W. B. Yeats's Country, one day I repeated aloud from memory Yeats's *The Song of Wandering Aengus* to the people in one of the pubs. How they became friendly to us! It is one of our unforgettable memories of twelve years ago.

"Ah! Yushiro, you should go alone, since you have several close friends there!" said she with an imploring shadow on her eyes.

In my mind's eye, many pleasant pictures come and pass. Life in the pursuit of illusions has ended. For us, the present moment itself is most important. It is nonsense, my going to Ireland alone.

Three weeks have passed and my baggage the size of 53x40x21(cm) remains even now as it was packed, still at the entrance hall.

第 2 部

Yoshiko, One Hundred and Three Years Old

"Who are you?" Yoshiko, my mother-in-law, asked me wearily.

"He is Yushiro-san, my husband, mummy," said Kyoko with a smile.

It was in the afternoon of the seventh day in March when we visited the Granny Komae Niban-kan where Yoshiko had lived more than five years.

She seemed to have fallen into a doze. We do not know what she was then dreaming about. Her face without a false tooth seemed to have caved in a little and strangely looked rather pretty. She had not been always senile. Sometimes she had been very clear. One week before, we had had a chat with her over the trifles of life when she recognized me clearly.

"I want to go back to my house," she said cheerlessly.

"The Care House is mummy's home," Kyoko said determinedly.

"I see," Yoshiko answered half-hopelessly.

There was a knock at the door and a stout and favorable nurse, Shoji-san, came in. It was the time for her to exchange the diaper covers. Suddenly, Yoshiko became lively and beamed a little. They were congenial with each other. We got

98

Memories and Ideas

out of the room for a while. The nurse finished her work soon and said that everything was OK.

"I felt refreshed, but I want to die. I am sorry for having lived so long," Yoshiko said to us and to herself in an apologetic tone. "That is a glorious nonsense." said I.

We could not imagine the inward world of one-hundred-and three-years-old woman. Time passed silently. Yoshiko seemed to be looking for something all the time. She was somehow ill at ease. Now and then, she talked nonsense. She had loved plants and flowers while she stayed at her own house.

Her veined hands had become slender little by little. The skin stained in purple color and the stain spread all over her body. Before my eyes Yoshiko was lying as she was. She was weak in sight, hard of hearing, could not chew any food and could not walk by herself.

Aging had cut off her selfishness and stout-heartedness. When I stayed there awhile with her, I could not but feel a little bored. She had no spiritual brilliance. The Meiji Era produced this kind of marionette woman who lacked having her own individuality. I wish she could have got a warmer heart. Until four months ago, she would throw her shoes at her neighbor when they seated side by side in the resting room. We often heard about her bold behavior. In those days she herself might have intended to show her own sense of independence as a woman.

99

第 2 部

Yoshiko, One Hundred and Four Years Old

"Hello! Mother, how are you?" I said to Yoshiko, my mother-in-law, merrily to the best of my ability.

"Yushiro-san? It is my birthday today." She beamed rather pleasantly.

It was in the morning of the fourth day of January when I called on the Granny Komae Niban-Kan where she had lived more than six years.

"Oh, you have a glorious memory." I remarked cheerfully and chanted.

"Happy birthday to you! Happy birthday to you!" though it was awkwardly out of tune.

Then I asked her, "How old are you?"

"I am twenty five years old." She said clearly with a smile.

Then, after knocking, Shoji-san, her favorite nurse, came in. Hearing the word 'twenty five,' she said, "How wonderful it is for you to be so young!"

"Akutsu-san (Yoshiko's surname), when you were twenty five years old, surely you had a nice secret, hadn't you?" She asked her brightly.

Yoshiko did not reply anything, and after a pause, she said feebly, "My foot is painful."

100

There seems no border between consciousness and unconsciousness. In the gap, however, in many cases, a person happens to disclose the essence of his or her inner character or personality. As for her, she lacks naivety and that makes me hesitate to continue with my next words. Did she wish to avoid the topic of old age? I wonder, what shall I say?

We can not see the world of unconsciousness. But the invisible is more important. We feel the sweetness of air, the softness of flowers, the warmth of nature and kindness of a person's sight.

She has had no vital force which drove her to an unknown world by nature.

"Which foot is painful?" asking her, Shoji-san was puzzled.

"Is this foot or, that?" She asked her pitiably, touching softly her ankles.

Suddenly I thought that long-in-bedded persons might have the death of a portion of the organism. A foot is the focus of it. Years would have caused her to lose her bearings. She is now in a fog.

This is the reality in which she lives. She is one hundred and four years old. She has lived as much as possible. Her veined hands have become terribly thin. Skin stained in purple, and the indelible blots have increased all over her body.

Aging is an uncertain journey.

I passed my hand over her painful foot, softly.

The sky is clear, but it is cold and windy.

第 2 部

Farewell to Yoshiko-san

Suddenly we had a call from Dr. S. who is associated with Granny Komae Niban-kan where Yoshiko had lived more than six years and now was one hundred and four years old. It was in the afternoon on the twenty-third day of April.

Kyoko has two elder brothers. She rang and told them how Yoshiko was. Several hours later, six persons including their wives of the brothers, gathered around Yoshiko. The average age was over eighty. Death was familiar to us all.

At that time, knocking on the door lightly, Shoji-san, her favorite nurse, came into the room and said to her softly; "Yoshiko-san, open your eyes as wide as possible, please."

Keeping a smile on her lips, in a tender gesture, she flashed a medical pencil torch to Yoshiko's right eye, while holding the eyelids open with two finger-tips of her right hand. Yoshiko had kept her eyes closed day and night recently. Her blood pressure was 82 and under 40. Oxygen in the blood was 102. Breathing frequency was 19 per minute. She had no excretion of urine.

Yoshiko had not accepted any food or drink for more than two weeks. Shoji-san says that energy of deglutition depends on how the pupil is. We have known when the pupil does not work actively, nutrition and drink one swallows may be liable

Memories and Ideas

to get into the lungs, not into the stomach.

In a moment, Shoji-san tilted her head in silence.

"Mother, Mother! We are here altogether around you, can you see us?" We said loudly to her. She reacted with a little blush, while her eyes remained closed. Her heart beat quickened, a teardrop ran down along her hollowed cheek.

"Yoshiko-san, how happy you are!" Saying so, Shoji-san wiped it tenderly with a piece of tissue paper.

I don't know if it is a happy tear or a regretful one.

After slight taps, Dr. S. who had treated her for over six years, came in.

"She has a strong life force which has kept her alive over two weeks without eating and drinking."

"But it is necessary for her to have someone wipe out the inside of her mouth carefully with wet sterilized gauze," and he added, "From now on, the aspect of affairs will worsen little by little."

However, until she breathed her last, someone would be beside her. We took turns one by one, and watched her attentively every day and night.

Two days later, during my turn, I gazed at her feet whose nails were delicately cracked as if they were little ripples on the edge of a river.

In the meantime, drowsiness attacked me. I heard a siren and dreamed of a strange car coming up to her, whose plate-number was "Shinagawa–830, A–14–58."

第 2 部

Haircut

"Could you cut my hair, if you are free?" I asked Kyoko reservedly, looking askance at her.

"Sure, uh-huh, maybe tomorrow, after tea time it is better," said she.

It was in the morning on the eighth day of September when I felt itchy, all of a sudden, everywhere in my head. Without my noticing, over two months had passed since I had my hair cut. Usually, she was to give me haircut every one month and a half, when she was in a cheerful mood.

I was in the beginning of my forties when I used to go to a barber's shop nearby the house. Whenever I returned, she said that the shortcut hair-style was unsuitable for me, and that it looked not like me but a different person. Moreover, she added that it was important for me to be always myself not only in hairstyle, but in neckties and casual clothes. Thus she became her husband's barber.

We have favorable hairdressing implements. Forty-five years ago, I taught at Rissho University near the JR Gotanda Station, she studied English Literature there in the graduate school. She was less than thirty years old and pretty. At that time, there seemed no awkward habit with her. We returned home together once a week. Nearby the station, we found a

104

Memories and Ideas

set of good barber's scissors in a shop.

Chuck, chuck, chuck—listening to the cutting sounds, I remembered our past good days. Every scene around and within us was fresh and vivid. It smelled of fresh coffee and milk mixed with a spiritual aristocracy there. They were some of Rembrandt's pictures with light and shade.

"Raise your head, a little more!" she said in a clear voice.

While she cut skillfully the side hair with the scissors, little by little, the hair fell on old newspapers that were spread on the floor. With a vinyl sheet covering my neck and shoulders, I sat down there, slightly bending forward with legs crossed.

"Oh, No! Don't sleep, Yushiro-san." she exclaimed.

I dreamt within a dream in the daylight. Silent crossing movements of scissors and comb as well as her old-warm scent, made me happy. Her way of working is very conscientious. Silent safety might have brought me a mild sleep. It has become one of my biggest pleasures for the short remaining life.

"Look! Your hair remains still half black and rich for your age," said she, joyfully.

"We always eat seaweed, small fish, protein of animals and vegetables." I told her in a small voice.

第 2 部

The Car for Ladies Only

It was nine o'clock in the morning on the fifteenth day of May when Kyoko and I caught an express train for Shinjuku at the Seijyogakuen-mae Station. Instinctively, we chose the car at the rear of the train.

There were very few persons who stood in the car. But almost all seats were occupied. I had a big umbrella for a stick and wore thin brown colored sun-glasses. Probably I looked a poor old man at the first glance.

I scarcely stood in front of a young girl who seemed twenty years old or so when I began to memorize some of my favorite English poetry by my heart with the eyes closed dimly. It was my custom to take advantage of the futile time.

"Please sit down," the girl said to me.

She kindly gave the seat to me with a smile. I thanked her with a silent bow. She moved smoothly to the opposite side and stood with her back towards me.

Silence reigned all around. No one spoke. Fresh air came in from open spaces in the windows. Everyone seemed to be enjoying themselves in the relaxed short time.

"Oh! It is funny. This is the car for exclusive use of ladies," Kyoko said to me in a secret voice.

"I didn't know they were running this kind of car until half

Memories and Ideas

past nine o'clock," she apologized to me.

"But it is OK. You are eighty-four years old. You look like a refined scholar, every inch of you. Please, stay as you are," she said calmly.

She remained standing as if she concealed me with her slender figure.

In a moment, I felt uneasy. With my eyes turned up, I looked around restlessly.

Nobody gazed at me. Many of them were reading books or newspapers without noticing me. Some of them were chatting or handling their little phones. One lady in the mid-40s, at some odd corner, smiled to me with the warm sympathy.

Office girls, students of university or high school, and wives with girl children—there were many kinds of women.

Why Kyoko did guide me to the car for exclusive use of ladies? She is a careful and honest woman. Yes, she knows my taste; I love the rear car always for no particular reason. She obeyed my taste first.

Time has past slowly. The first or second rush hours passed.

This was a scene with figures of various kinds of women except me.

The young girl, who offered her seat to me, got off at the third station called Kyodo where stood a famous women's university. She may belong to it. She left an aroma behind.

When we reached Shinjuku, it was half past nine.

第 2 部

Kyoko's Birthday

"Congratulations, this is for you, Kyoko," saying this, I handed her a little bamboo bonsai as well as a bouquet of Siberian lilies.

"How happy I am, thank you very much indeed, Yushiro-san," said she.

"But how you could remember my birthday, it is unbelievable!" she added with uncontrollable joy.

"It is the first time for me to receive your gift on my birthday since we got married," she told me with deep emotion.

I was sure, of course, that I had presented her with something memorable several times before, but I suppressed the mutterings within me. I felt happy seeing her naïve smiles, lively expression and pleasant movements.

It was in the later afternoon of the eighth day of October.

I remember; one hour ago, I drove my bicycle to nearby Odakyu OX where they had a domestic flower shop. Entering it, I noticed a heart-shaped bonsai of little bamboos. The size of about ten centimeters square and the same measure in height was appreciatory. The light green and tiny leaves were pretty. The color of the plate which was placed at the bottom of the bamboo roots was black, and into which we were to pour ample water every day. It seemed to be suitable for the

108

Memories and Ideas

large boot cupboard of our entrance hall, whose wooden color was yellow-golden. Moreover the heart-shaped bonsai was apparently warm and attractive for us.

In addition to it, the bouquet consisted of two pieces of white Siberian lilies that had nine buds each. Four of them were open, and others were beginning to open, but the rest were almost closed. It is said that many buds suggest possibilities in the future. White lilies show not only purity but also aristocracy. Yellow, pink and any other colors are out of the question. Bamboo is the symbol of strength as well as simplicity and transparency which are indispensable in our daily life. These are the significant presents for her. I loved both of them at first sight.

Unconsciously I had thought back about fifty years ago when we got married. It was the season of cherry blossoms. She was twenty-three years old and I was thirty-six years old. As if in a dream, half a century passed. Now I am eighty-six years old.

Recently Kyoko became seamed with shadowy wrinkles on her face and neck. Her every movement is slow and she is forgetful of things. Half a year later, we will have our fiftieth wedding party.

I was not aware of any particular reason or any intention to celebrate our ordinary occasion. I just wanted to show my modest frame of mind to her on her birthday.

109

第３部
Part Three

漢詩のほそみち
──春・夏・秋・冬──
（七言絶句　習作）

第一章　春

新春　四題

I （上平・一東）

東風萬里五雲中	東風（とうふう）　万里　五雲（ごうん）の中
辛卯歳朝初旭紅	辛卯（しんう）　歳朝　初旭紅（しょきょくこう）なり
物換星移身好在	物換わり　星移るも　身は好在（こうざい）
陶然重盞氣蓬蓬	陶然（とうぜん）　盞（さん）を重ね　気蓬々たり

◆**大意**　春風につつまれ瑞雲が浮かぶ。元日の早朝、紅色の朝日が昇る。一年経った、わたくしは健康。うっとり屠蘇の杯を重ね、気力が湧く。

◆**注**　東風＝春風。五雲＝瑞雲。卯＝午前六時。辛卯＝早朝。歳朝＝元旦。蓬蓬（ほうほう）＝盛んなさま。

第3部

Ⅱ （下平・七陽）

乾坤春色迎初陽　　　乾坤　春色　初陽を迎う

草屋爐邊椒酒香　　　草屋　炉辺　椒酒香し

宿志老來猶抱處　　　宿志　老来　猶抱く処

欣然欲遂世塵忘　　　欣然　遂げんと欲し　世塵忘る

◆**大意**　天地に春色が漲り、初日の出を迎えた。慎ましい我
　が家の炉辺、屠蘇の香。老いてなお成し遂げたい仕事があ
　る。よしやるぞ、奮い立つと雑念は去る。

◆**注**　乾坤＝天地。草屋＝自分の家。爐邊＝火のあるところ、
　居間。椒酒＝屠蘇。椒は山椒。老来＝老いること。

Ⅲ （上平・十一真）

履端淑氣曙光新　　　履端の淑気　曙光新たなり

盎盎五雲天地春　　　央々たる五雲　天地の春

閑酌屠蘇清硯海　　　閑酌の屠蘇　硯海を清め

揮來試筆絶心塵　　　揮い来たる試筆　心塵を絶つ

◆**大意**　清らかな正月。曙光が新鮮。瑞雲が湧き、天地は将に春。屠蘇を酌み、黒々した硯の墨と対決。書き初めの筆を振るう、心が引き締まり雑念は去る。

◆**注**　履端＝年の初め。淑＝深い、清い。盎盎＝盛んなさま。硯海＝墨汁を海と捉えると──硯の水が海となる。

Ⅳ（上平・十灰）

五雲萬里曙光催	五雲　万里　曙光催し
華髪迎春意自恢	華髪　春を迎え　意自ずから恢し
椒酒一杯微醉處	椒酒　一杯　微酔の処
新詩忽就笑顔開	新詩　忽ち就り　笑顔開く

◆**大意**　天地に寿ぎが漲っている。白髪も色艶よく、正月は心が自然に広くなる。屠蘇で口を潤すとほんのり酔ってしまう。湧きでるように詩が生まれ、微笑がうかぶ。

◆**注**　華髪＝色艶のいい白髪。恢＝ひろし。

第3部

早春　二題

Ⅰ　（上平・四支）

輕寒欲去暗香吹	軽寒　去らんと欲し　暗香吹く
欣見庭前梅一枝	欣び見る　庭前　梅一枝
依杖出門春尚淺	杖に依り門を出づれば　春尚浅し
早鶯舌澁樹陰姿	早鶯　舌渋る　樹陰の姿

◆**大意**　寒さも薄らぎ梅香が微かに漾う。心嬉しく庭に眼をやると、一枝の蕾が膨らんでいる。杖曳いて門をでる、春はまだ浅い。鶯は未だ鳴かず、梅樹の陰に姿を隠している。

◆**注**　暗香＝どこからとなく来るかおり。早鶯＝幼いうぐいす。

Ⅱ　（下平・一先）

暗香何處嫩寒天	暗香　何れの処ぞ　嫩寒の天
林下徘徊一朶妍	林下　徘徊すれば　一朶妍なり
冷艷依稀微月下	冷艶　依稀たり　微月の下
佳人如畫寫吟箋	佳人　画くが如く　吟箋に写さん

116

漢詩のほそみち――春・夏・秋・冬――

◆**大意** 梅の香が何処からともなく漾う薄ら寒い空。梅林の徘徊。言いようもなく美しい一輪の梅花。微月のもと冷艶な姿を少々見せている。絵に描くように早春の佳人を美しく詩に歌おう。

◆**注** 嫩寒（どんかん）＝春の薄ら寒さ。妍（けん）＝美しい、艶めかしい。依稀（いき）＝ぼんやり見える。吟箋＝詩をしたためる美しい紙。

立春　二題

I（下平・一先）

東風料峭夕陽前	東風　料峭（りょうしょう）　夕陽の前
疎影兩三春可憐	疎影　両三　春憐れむ可し
細細清香林下路	細々たる清香　林下の路
佳辰此景寫吟箋	佳辰（かしん）の此の景　吟箋に写さん

◆**大意** 厳しい春風、夕陽の前。ちらほら咲き始める梅花。まだ可憐な早春。微かな清香の漂う林下の径。素晴らしいこの景色を手元の手帳に詩でうたいたい。

◆**注** 料峭（りょうしょう）＝きびしい。両三＝ちらほら。佳辰＝恵まれた、素晴らしい。

117

第3部

Ⅱ （上平・四支）

庭前日午雨絲絲	庭前　日午（にちご）　雨絲々たり
數朶梅花含涙姿	数朶（すうだ）の梅花　涙を含む姿あり
天地春回生暖氣	天地　春は回り　暖気を生ず
爐邊煎茗獨題詩	炉辺　茗（みょう）を煎て　独り詩を題す

◆**大意**　細雨の降りつづく真昼の庭。梅花数枝、濡れて可憐。
天地に春が訪れ、暖気が漂う。茶でも淹れ詩をうたおう。

◆**注**　日午＝まひる。朶（だ）＝垂れさがる枝。茗＝茶。爐邊＝食
事する部屋位の意味。

探梅　三題

Ⅰ （上平・四支）

殘寒獨步默鶯児	残寒　独り歩めば　鶯児黙し
林下探梅一好枝	林下の探梅　一好枝（いちこうし）
聞得幽香春尚淺	幽香　聞き得たるも　春尚浅し
騷人何恨蕊開遲	騒人（そうじん）何ぞ恨まん　蕊開くこと遅きを

漢詩のほそみち──春・夏・秋・冬──

◆**大意**　残寒の中の独り歩き。鶯も啼かない。探梅。林下に蕾膨らませている好枝がある。仄かに匂う。春はまだ浅い。待ち遠しいが、蕾のほころびるのが遅れても恨みはしない。

◆**注**　騒人＝詩人、自分。

Ⅱ（下平・八庚）

滿林梅花白紅英	満林　梅花　白紅の英
脈脈清香歩歩輕	脈々たる清香　歩々軽し
枝上早聞鶯語滑	枝上早くも聞く　鶯語滑らかなるを
遊人索句忘歸程	遊人　句を索め　帰程を忘る

◆**大意**　美しい紅梅、白梅が出番を待っている。清香のなか足取り軽く林下を歩く。枝上に早や滑らかな鶯の啼き声。詩句をあれこれ考えているとつい帰りを忘れる。

◆**注**　遊人＝自分のこと。

119

第 3 部

Ⅲ （下平・六麻）

探梅曳杖影横斜　　探梅　杖を曳けば　影横斜

破蕾一枝三五花　　蕾を破り　一枝　三五の花

冷艶恍然朧月下　　冷艶　恍然　朧月の下

清香馥郁自無邪　　清香　馥郁　自らに邪無し

◆**大意**　杖を曳いて梅を探すと、枝の横斜に会う。なかに蕾
を綻ばせ、ちらほら花を咲かせようとする一枝を見る。う
っとりその冷艶な姿に見とれ佇む微月の下。清香が馥郁と
漂い、心洗われる気持ちになる。

看梅 （下平・八庚）

梅林曳杖一鶯鳴　　梅林　杖を曳けば　一鶯鳴く

破蕾枝頭春意盈　　蕾を破る　枝頭　春意盈つ

馥郁清香籠地好　　馥郁たる清香　地に籠めて好し

遊人恍惚愛花精　　遊人　恍惚　花精を愛す

漢詩のほそみち——春・夏・秋・冬——

◆ **大意**　杖を曳き梅林を歩む。鶯の鳴き声。枝先に蕾を破る早咲きの梅の花。春がそこまで来ている。馥郁とした清らな香。辺りいちめん立ち込めている。何とも云えない心地良さ。花の精をうっとり愛するわたくし。

◆ **注**　花精＝花の妖精・精霊。

春雨　三題

I （上平・五微）

書帷半濕冷春衣	書帷　半ば湿し　冷やかなり春衣
庭院冥冥緑正肥	庭院冥々　緑正に肥ゆ
奈此閑愁謀小酌	此の閑愁を奈せん　小酌を謀る
嫩寒侵座遠鐘微	嫩寒　座を侵し　遠鐘微なり

◆ **大意**　湿気を帯びてきた書斎のカーテン。春雨にわたくしの衣はひんやりする。庭はくらいが、草も緑色を帯びてきた。春の愁いの遣る瀬なさ。酒でも飲もう。薄ら寒さが腰の辺りに忍び寄る。微かに遠鐘が聞こえる。

◆ **注**　書幃＝書斎の幃。冥冥＝くらいこと。奈＝いかんせん。

第3部

Ⅱ （上平・四支）

一簾膏雨草離離　　一簾の膏雨　草離々たり

潤物却知春恨滋　　物を潤すも却って知る　春恨滋し

滿地落花門巷寂　　満地の落花　門巷寂たり

嫩寒無那使人悲　　嫩寒　那無し　人をして悲しましむ

◆**大意**　恵みの雨が簾越しに降っている。草はここかしこに
生い茂る。慈雨は万物を潤すが、春の愁いは尽きない。無
残なり満地の落花。ひっそりした門。薄ら寒さが物悲しい。

◆**注**　一簾膏雨＝簾越しに見る雨。膏雨＝時に応じて百穀を
潤すよい雨。離離＝ばらばらに乱れて繁るさま。門巷＝門。

Ⅲ （上平・五微）

春陰獨坐鎖蓬扉　　春陰　独坐　蓬扉を鎖す

細雨蕭蕭紅欲肥　　細雨　蕭々　紅肥えんと欲す

静聴淋鈴書院寂　　静かに聴く淋鈴　書院寂たり

黄昏一望遠村微　　黄昏　一望すれば　遠村微なり

漢詩のほそみち──春・夏・秋・冬──

◆**大意**　花ぐもりの日に独り坐し、草繁る門を閉ざす。もの
　寂しい風まじりの細かい雨がしとしと降る。色づく草。書
　斎で風鈴の音を聴く。襲いかかる寂寞。黄昏どきに遠望す
　れば、微かに村が見える。

◆**注**　春陰＝花ぐもり。蓬扉＝草茫茫の扉。蕭蕭＝風のもの
　　　　　　　　　　　　　　　　　　　しょうしょう
　寂しく吹く声。淋＝寂しいこと。
　りん

春夜（上平・十一真）

今宵寂寂落花頻　　　今宵　寂々　落花頻りなり
　　　　　　　　　　　　　　　　　　しき

小院無人愁更新　　　小院　人無く　愁更に新たなり

東帝伴寒如有意　　　東帝　寒を伴う　意有るが如し
　　　　　　　　　とうてい

千金雅調不相親　　　千金の雅調　相い親しまず

◆**大意**　もの寂しい今夕。頻りに落花の気配。書斎には唯独
　　　　　　　　　　　　　　　　　　けはい
　り。愁いはいっそう深まる。春の女神が寒さを連れてくる
　のは何か意味があるようだ。今宵は春宵一刻値千金のコト
　バが相応しくない。

◆**注**　小院＝書斎。東帝＝春の女神。千金雅調＝春宵一刻値
　千金（蘇軾「春夜」）。

123

第3部

春雪　二題

I （下平・八庚）

天寒曉起四望清	天寒く　曉起すれば　四望清し
如夢庭前玉樹生	夢の如く　庭前　玉樹生ず
凍雀悄然春尚淺	凍雀　悄然　春尚浅し
連肩軒下寂無聲	肩を連ね　軒下　寂として声無し

◆**大意**　暁の天は寒い。起きて見る。辺りはいちめん清らかな雪。夢のような庭の玉樹。雀たちは凍りついて悄然としている。春は未だ浅い。彼らは軒下に肩を連ね、ひっそり。鳴こうとしない。

◆**注**　四望＝四方。

II （下平・一先）

霏霏曉雪畫中天	霏々たる　暁雪　画中の天
小院妝成玉樹鮮	小院　妝成り　玉樹鮮やかなり
枝上春禽猶舌凍	枝上の　春禽　猶舌は凍り
殘寒料峭托詩篇	残寒　料峭　詩篇に托す

◆**大意** 降り続ける暁の雪。正に一幅の絵だ。雪化粧の庭の玉樹たち。見るも鮮やか。枝に留る小鳥たちは囀らない。残寒は厳しく、却って詩情が湧く。

◆**注** 霏霏＝雪の盛んに降るさま。小院＝庭。妝＝化粧、装い。

春宵 二題

I （上平・五微）

春宵閑聴雨聲微	春宵　閑かに聴く　雨声微なるを
潤物霏霏紅欲肥	物を潤し霏々たり　紅肥えんと欲す
門巷残寒人懶出	門巷　残寒　人出づるに懶し
兀頭獨坐戀芳霏	兀頭　独り坐して　芳霏を恋う

◆**大意** 春の宵に万物を潤す微かな雨の音をきく。草は盛んに繁ろうとしている。寒さが残り、出かけるのは億劫。禿げ頭の老人は独り座し、ひたすら花の咲くのを待つ。

◆**注** 兀頭＝禿げ頭。芳霏＝芳香の立ち昇るさま。霏＝きり（霧）、もや（霧）。

第 3 部

Ⅱ（上平・五微）

柳條青翠似成幃　　柳条は　青翠　幃を成すに似て

漠漠東郊草又肥　　漠々たる　東郊　草又肥ゆ

入夜軒頭誰叩戶　　夜に入り　軒頭　誰か戸を叩く

少間傾耳雨聲微　　少間　耳を傾ければ　雨声微なり

◆**大意**　柳の枝は薄緑色のカーテンのよう。漠々とした春の
　野辺。草が茂ろうとしている。夜、誰か軒を叩くような気
　配。しばらく耳澄ませ聞く。微かな雨の音である。

◆**注**　柳条＝柳の枝葉。幃＝とばり。東郊＝春の野辺。小間
　＝暫くの間。

春宵歩月（上平・十三元）

清遊半日月黄昏　　清遊　半日　月黄昏

形影朦朧情自存　　形影　朦朧　情自ずから存す

點點梅花春似畫　　点々たる　梅花　春画に似たり

誰知正是別乾坤　　誰か知らん　正に是　別乾坤

漢詩のほそみち──春・夏・秋・冬──

◆**大意**　清遊半日。何時の間にか夕暮れとなり月が出てきた。月影とわたくしの影。何れも朦朧としてこころが通じ合っているようだ。梅花が点綴し、春は一幅の絵である。誰が知ろうこの別世界の光景を。

春日郊行　三題

I　（上平・十灰）

東郊風暖獨徘徊	東郊　風暖かく　独り徘徊す
草徑水邊無俗埃	草径　水辺　俗埃無し
春日遲遲吟杖遠	春日　遅々として　吟杖遠し
野花戲蝶暮鐘催	野花　蝶に戯れ　暮鐘催す

◆**大意**　風の温かい春の野辺。独り徘徊。水辺の草生える小径には俗塵がない。遅々とした春の日。のんびり、遠くまで散策。野原に咲く花に蝶が戯れ、夕暮の鐘の音が聞こえる。

◆**注**　埃＝ほこり、塵。

127

第3部

Ⅱ （上平・四支）

韶光風暖鳥先知	韶光　風暖かく　鳥先ず知る
告我東郊芳草滋	我に告ぐ　東郊　芳草滋しと
灼灼夭桃花亂落	灼々（しゃくしゃく）たる　夭桃（ようとう）　花乱れ落つ
歸程失處夕陽遲	帰程　失う処　夕陽遅し

◆**大意**　風暖かく春めく光は鳥たちが先ず知る。彼らは教え
てくれる。野辺には草が匂い茂っていますよと。出かける
と咲き乱れ、落ちている桃の花。帰る氣もしない。だが夕
陽はかなり傾いてきた。

◆**注**　韶光＝春の光。灼灼（しゃくしゃく）＝花の盛んなる貌。夭桃（ようとう）＝若く美
しい桃の木。若い女性の色香に例える。

Ⅲ （上平・十一眞）

夜來細細雨連晨	夜来　細々　雨晨（しん）に連なる
柳眼将萌草色匀	柳眼　将に萌えんとし　草色匀う（ととの）
風拂殘雲生暖氣	風は残雲を払い　暖気を生ず
桃花灼灼一村春	桃花　灼々　一村の春

漢詩のほそみち——春・夏・秋・冬——

◆**大意**　夜半から降り始めた細い雨。明け方になっても止まない。柳の芽が萌えでようとし、辺りの草たちも色づいてきた。春風が冬の名残の雲を吹き払い、暖かさが膨らみはじめている。桃の花が咲き誇るある村の一風景。

◆**注**　夜来＝夜半。晨＝あさがた。柳眼＝柳の枝葉。匀＝ととのう。

水畔摘蔬（上平・六魚）

水邊曳杖午風疎　　水辺　杖を曳けば　午風疎なり

欲摘春蔬歩自徐　　春蔬を摘まんと欲すれば　歩自ずから徐なり

殘雪汀頭芹蓼緑　　残雪の汀頭　芹 蓼<ruby>緑<rt>きんりょう</rt></ruby>に

籠中香滿意安如　　籠中　香満ちて　意は安如

◆**大意**　春先、水辺に杖を曳いて散策。昼の風は殆どない。春野菜を摘もうとゆっくり歩く。雪の残る水際。せり、たでは緑に色づいている。たくさん摘む。籠は一杯になり、その何とも云えない新芽の香にこころは安らぐ。

◆**注**　疎＝まばら。<ruby>蔬<rt>そ</rt></ruby>＝あおもの野菜。歩＝ほ。あゆみ。徐＝おもむろ。<ruby>汀<rt>てい</rt></ruby>＝なぎさ。<ruby>芹<rt>きん</rt></ruby>＝せり。<ruby>蓼<rt>りょう</rt></ruby>＝たで。<ruby>意安如<rt>い あんじょ</rt></ruby>＝こころは安らぐ。

129

第3部

春日帰郷 （上平・四支）

歸郷村巷短筇移　　郷に帰れば　村巷に　短筇移す

鳥語嗒嗒聞舊枝　　鳥語　嗒々　旧枝に聞く

駘蕩春風吹袂暖　　駘蕩たる春風　袂を吹いて暖かく

依然勝景憶童時　　依然たる　勝景　童時を憶う

◆**大意**　故郷に帰り、村のここかしこ、杖を曳いて歩く。鳥
たちが楽しそうに昔見慣れた枝上で囀っている。まさに春
風駘蕩。風が袂を吹きぬけて暖かい。辺りの風景は、昔の
ままである。幼少時代が懐しい。

◆**注**　村巷＝村。筇＝杖。嗒嗒＝鳥の声が和らいで遠くから
聞こえるさま。駘蕩＝春景色ののどかなさま。

春日即事 （上平・十一真）

清明時節鳥聲頻　　清明の時節　鳥声頻りなり

靄靄東郊天地春　　靄々たる東郊　天地の春

紅雨粉粉如夢裡　　紅雨　粉々　夢裡の如し

閑愁兀兀踏青人　　閑愁　兀々　踏青の人

◆**大意**　四月の初め、鳥の声がしきりにする。雲、霞が棚引く春の野辺。早々と散る紅の花弁の雨。夢の世界である。この春愁にみちた野遊びの楽しさ。

◆**注**　清明＝四月五日頃。靄靄（あいあい）＝雲や霞の集まり棚引くさま。兀兀（こつこつ）＝動かないさま。踏青＝春日郊外のあそび。

看櫻（千鳥が淵）三題

I　（下平・六麻）

韶光正誘萬櫻花　　韶光　正に誘う　万桜花

仰見香雲獨醉華　　仰ぎ見る　香雲　独り華に酔う

鳥語喈喈林下路　　鳥語　喈々　林下の路

徘徊紅雨夕陽斜　　徘徊　紅雨　夕陽斜めなり

◆**大意**　春光に誘われ、桜花は満開。芳香を放つ華（はな）の粋（いき）な美しさに陶酔してしまう。鳥たちの楽しそうに囀る桜下の小径。行きつ戻りつ、紅の花弁の雨に降られている裡に、夕陽が射してきた。

◆**注**　韶光＝春の光。香雲＝桜花。

131

第3部

Ⅱ（下平・六麻）

櫻堤十里淡濃霞　　桜堤　十里　淡濃の霞

碧落描紅萬朶花　　碧落に紅を描く　万朶の花

鳥語喈喈如有意　　鳥語　喈々　意有るが如し

倣君騒客更稱華　　君に倣い　騒客　更に華を稱めん

◆**大意**　桜咲く堤は長く続き、濃淡の花弁が霞状に広がっている。青空に映しだされる沢山の桜の紅の色。鳥たちの楽しそうなお喋りには何か意味がありそう。君たちに倣ってわたくしも、この美しい桜を精いっぱい褒め讃えよう。

◆**注**　碧落＝あおぞら。碧空。稱＝ほめる。騒客＝わたくし。

Ⅲ（上平・四支）

芳菲十里好題詩　　芳菲　十里　好し詩を題せん

碧落誇紅千萬枝　　碧落　紅を誇る　千万の枝

人語近聞如夢裡　　人語を近くに聞けども　夢裡の如し

櫻花映水更清奇　　桜花　水に映じて　更に清奇なり

◆**大意** 辺りいちめんに拡がる桜またさくら。詩にうたいたい。碧空にその美を誇る無数の枝々。人びとの賛嘆の声が夢うつつにきこえる。お堀の水に映る桜は清らかで美しい。

春愁　二題

Ⅰ　（上平・十一真）

幽庭追日草如茵	幽庭　日を追い　草茵の如し
已過清明欲老春	已に清明を過ぎ　老いんと欲する春
繚亂飛花無限恨	繚乱の飛花　無限の恨み
鶯聲尚滑促吟神	鶯声　尚滑らかに　吟神を促す

◆**大意** 我が家の庭。日増しに草が茵のように生えてきた。春も四月五日を過ぎると老いていく。咲き誇っていた数々の花たちが散っていく。無限の恨みが残る。晩春の滑らかな鶯の鳴き声。歌心をそそられる。

◆**注** 茵＝しとね。吟神＝歌ごころ。

133

第3部

Ⅱ（下平・九青）

斜風細雨入窓櫺	斜風　細雨　窓櫺に入り
門掩残寒暗小庭	門は残寒に掩われ　小庭暗し
一脈閑愁思往事	一脈の閑愁　往事を思う
銜杯只見古苔青	杯を銜み　只見る　古苔の青きを

◆**大意**　風を伴い斜めに吹きつける細い雨が窓格子に当たる。門は残寒に蔽われ、庭は薄暗い。わたくしの心は春愁に囚われ、過ぎ去った過去を懐かしく思い出す。酒を含み無心に、庭の古びた蒼い苔を眺めやる。

◆**注**　窓櫺＝窓格子。杯＝盃、酒。銜む＝のむ。

徂春　五題

Ⅰ（上平・十一眞）

斜風細雨落花晨	斜風　細雨　落花の晨
蝶怨鶯愁緑早匀	蝶怨み　鶯愁い　緑早くも匀う
九十春光茫似夢	九十の春光　茫として夢に似たり
東君已老祝融隣	東君　已に老い　祝融隣なる

漢詩のほそみち――春・夏・秋・冬――

◆**大意** 風混じりの雨が細く斜めに降り、朝から花が散る。逝く春を蝶怨み鶯は愁う。草木は緑の衣替えに忙しい。三ケ月は茫として夢のように過ぎ春はすでに老い、夏の神はもうすぐ隣にきている。

◆**注** 九十の春光＝春三ケ月。祝<ruby>融<rt>しゅくゆう</rt></ruby>＝夏の神。

Ⅱ （下平・六麻）

閑愁誰識惜殘花	閑愁誰か識らん　残花を惜しむを
滿地香泥憐更加	満地の香泥　憐れみ更に加わる
春草萋萋翻有恨	春草　萋々　<ruby>翻<rt>かえ</rt></ruby>って恨み有り
無爲爐畔獨煎茶	無為　炉畔　独り茶を煎る

◆**大意** 逝く春。僅かに残る花。この言い知れぬ愁い。誰が分かってくれよう。辺り一面に散る泥まみれの花弁。愁いは一層深まる。草の茂るのが恨めしい。為すことなく独り居間で茶を淹れる。この侘びしさ。

◆**注** <ruby>萋萋<rt>さいさい</rt></ruby>＝草のさかんなるさま。翻＝かえって。炉畔＝居間。

135

第3部

Ⅲ （下平・十一尤）

紅飛紫散不勝愁　　紅飛　紫散　愁いに勝えず

回駕青皇去不留　　駕を回らし青皇　去って留まらず

芳事闌殘春寂寞　　芳事闌残　春寂寞

斜風細雨緑陰稠　　斜風　細雨　緑陰稠し

- **◆大意**　紅紫さまざまな色の花たち。みな散って愁いは深まるばかり。春の女神は去っていった。逝く春。春闌けて、寂寞の感に耐えない。風を含んだ細い雨が斜めに降りかかる。緑の木陰が色濃くなっている。

- **◆注**　青皇＝春を司る神・青帝・東帝・東皇ともいう。闌＝半ば過ぎ。寂寞＝落寞＝索寞、さびしく静か。

Ⅳ （下平・六麻）

杏花零落亂如麻　　杏花　零落　乱れて麻の如し

寂寞庭前雀浴沙　　寂寞たり　庭前　雀沙を浴ぶ

憐我傷心春有恨　　憐れむ我が傷心　春に恨み有り

老鶯不語夕陽斜　　老鶯　語らず　夕陽斜めなり

漢詩のほそみち──春・夏・秋・冬──

◆**大意**　杏の花は麻のように枯れしほんでいる。寂しくなった庭先。雀たちの戯れの砂浴び。逝く春を惜しみ心は傷む。鶯も老いて鳴かない。斜めに差す夕陽が愛おしい。

◆**注**　零落＝枯れしほむこと（草の枯れるのが零、木の枯れるのが落）。沙＝砂。傷心＝惜春の情。

V （上平・十一眞）

閑愁自起落花春	閑愁　自ずから起こる　落花の春
坐見幽庭緑已匀	坐して見る　幽庭　緑已に匀う
滿地香泥痕尚止	滿地の香泥　痕尚止め
暖風習習鳥聲頻	暖風　習々　鳥声頻りなり

◆**大意**　静かな愁いがおのずから湧きおこるのが落花の春であろう。坐して見る静かな庭。緑が薄っすらと芽生え始めている。到るところに花の色香の痕跡をとどめている。暖かい風が吹き、鳥たちの鳴き声がしきりにきこえる。

◆**注**　已＝すでに。匀＝ととのう。習習＝春風の和らぎ舒るさま。

137

第3部

落花有感　二題

I　（下平・八庚）

徂春今日半陰晴　　徂春　今日　陰晴を半ばす

萬紫千紅欲盡榮　　万紫　千紅　尽きんと欲する栄（えい）

昨夜狂風無頼荐　　昨夜　狂風　無頼荐（しき）りなり

流鶯不語獨傷情　　流鶯　語らず　独り情を傷ましむ

　◆**大意**　過ぎゆく春。晴れたり曇ったり。紅と紫いろに充ちた春の盛りは尽きようとしている。昨夜は風が吹き荒れた。鶯は鳴かずに飛び去る。わたくしは独り愁いに沈む。

　◆**注**　徂＝過ぎ行く。栄＝栄えること。荐＝かさねる。

II　（上平・十一眞）

三春将盡暗愁新　　三春将に尽きんとし　暗愁新たなり

細雨應憐花作塵　　細雨応に憐れむべし　花（はな）塵となるを

一路香泥都似夢　　一路の香泥　都（すべ）て夢に似たり

榮華忽變四時巡　　栄華　忽ち変じ　四時巡る

漢詩のほそみち――春・夏・秋・冬――

◆**大意**　春は正に尽きようとし、愁いが新たに湧く。細い雨。花が散って塵になるのは観るも哀れである。繚乱の花たちが泥土と化す。正に夢である。春の栄華も忽ち移ろい、時は過ぎて行く。

◆**注**　三春＝1～3の三ヶ月、九十日の春。塵＝ちり。都＝すべて。

第3部

第二章　夏

緑陰（下平・一先）

薫風脈脈雨餘天	薫風　脈々　雨余の天
檐鐵丁東疎俗縁	檐鉄（えんてつ）　丁東　俗縁疎なり
僻巷深居無客訪	僻巷の深居　客の訪う（おとな）無し
一庭新緑色逾鮮	一庭の新緑　色 愈（いよいよ） 鮮やかなり

◆**大意**　五月。心地よい風がそよぐ雨上がり。風鈴がチリン
チリン鳴って憂世離れしている。田舎住居のわたくしの處
にきてくれる人はいない。庭の新緑はいよいよ鮮やかにな
っている。

◆**注**　脈脈＝絶え間のないさま。雨餘＝雨上がり。檐鐵（えんてつ）＝風
鈴。丁東＝とうとう、風鈴などの触れあう声。僻巷＝街は
ずれ。逾＝愈＝いよいよ。

140

漢詩のほそみち——春・夏・秋・冬——

緑陰品茗　二題

I （上平・十三元）

小園竹蔭別乾坤	小園の竹蔭は　別乾坤
閑坐煎茶鳥語繁	閑坐　茶を煎れば　鳥語繁し
沸沸松濤恰如和	沸々たる松涛　恰も和するが如し
風鈴午搨忘塵煩	風鈴の午搨　塵煩を忘る

◆**大意**　庭の竹林は別世界。閑坐して茶を煎ると鳥たちが来
てしきりに囀る。茶を淹れる湯の沸く音が鳥声と互いに和
しているようだ。昼下がり風鈴の音。椅子に腰掛けて寛ぐ。
煩わしい世塵を忘れる。

◆**注**　小園＝家の庭。竹蔭＝竹のかげ。沸＝ふつ、煮えたぎ
る。涛＝とう、波だつこと。沸々松涛＝茶を淹れる湯がわ
くこと。午搨＝昼下がりに寄り掛かる椅子。

141

第3部

Ⅱ （上平・十三元）

疎簾搖動緑陰繁	疎簾　揺動し　緑陰繁し
習習薰風度小軒	習々たる　薫風　小軒を度る
一椀新茶香郁郁	一椀の新茶　香郁々
枯腸沾處忘塵煩	枯腸　沾う処　塵煩を忘る

◆**大意**　粗い目の簾が揺れ動く。緑陰の波また波。薫風が我
が家を吹きぬける。一椀の新茶の馥郁とした香が漂う。乾
いている腸が沾うと、塵の世の煩わしさなど忘れてしまう。

◆**注**　習習＝風の音の形容。小軒＝我が家。度＝わたる。郁
郁＝香気の盛んなるさま。枯腸＝水分不足の腸。喉の渇き。
沾＝潤す。塵煩＝憂き世の煩わしさ。

漢詩のほそみち――春・夏・秋・冬――

初夏　二題

Ⅰ　（下平・一先）

雨過如拭麥秋天	雨過ぎて　拭うが如し　麦秋の天
永日東郊水滿田	永日　東郊　水田（みず）に満つ
閣閣蛙聲農事急	閣々（こうこう）たる　蛙声（あせい）　農事急なり
薫風吹緑誘清漣	薫風　緑を吹き　清漣を誘う

◆大意　雨は拭い去るように止み、初夏の明るい空模様となった。野辺の水田には終日、水が満々と湛えられている。蛙の鳴き声はかまびすしく、農作業の繁忙さを告げている。薫風が田の面（も）を吹き渡り、清らかな漣を誘う。

◆注　麦秋＝初夏。閣閣（こうこう）（かか、かうかう）＝蛙の鳴き声の形容。

Ⅱ　（上平・五微）

百花落盡筍将肥	百花落ち尽し　筍（しゅん）将に肥えんとす
新樹陽光緑四圍	新樹　陽光　緑四（よ）もを囲む
杜宇何邊出門處	杜宇　何れの辺ぞ　門を出づる処
薫風一路染吟衣	薫風一路　吟衣を染む

143

第3部

◆**大意** 春の花たちはみな散り果てた。竹の子が大きくなろうとしている。陽光に輝く樹々の新緑が四方を囲む。不如帰が門の外の何処かで鳴いている。我が衣に初夏のそよ風が染みこみ、歌ごころが起こる。

◆**注** 筍＝しゅん、たけのこ。杜宇＝とう、ほととぎす。もと蜀王望帝の名。その魂、化して杜鵑（ほととぎす）になるという伝説による。

初夏偶成（上平・四支）

麥秋小院草離離	麦秋　小院　草離々たり
可愛榴花紅滿枝	愛す可し　榴花（こうえだ）　紅枝に満つ
風搖疎簾心氣爽	風は疎簾を揺るがし　心気爽やかに
新茶一啜好題詩	新茶一啜（せつ）　好し詩を題せん

◆**大意** 初夏。隠者の家の庭。草がばらばらに乱れ茂っている。柘榴の木の枝に紅い実が沢山ついている。可愛らしい。簾が風に揺れ、心は爽やか。新茶を啜る。良い詩が書けそうだ。

◆**注** 麦秋＝麦収穫の季節、初夏。草離離＝草の生い茂るさま。榴花＝柘榴。啜（せつ）＝「てつ」とも読む。すする意。

漢詩のほそみち――春・夏・秋・冬――

緑陰読書　二題

I （上平・十三元）

薫風習習緑陰繁	薫風　習々　緑陰繁し
簷鐵丁當僻巷軒	簷鐵　丁当　僻巷の軒
獨誦詩篇心氣爽	独誦の詩篇　心気爽やかに
江湖至楽坐邊存	江湖の至楽　坐辺に存す

◆**大意**　そよ風が吹き益々色濃くなる緑の木陰。愛おしい。
　風鈴が鳴るチリンチリン。隠者の住む田舎の家。何篇かの
　詩を誦する。気分爽快。世を捨てた人間の楽しみはこうい
　う処にある。

◆**注**　丁當＝風鈴の鳴る声。江湖＝世捨人のいる所の譬え。
　坐辺＝身の周り。

145

第3部

Ⅱ （下平・十一尤）

幽窓静坐緑陰稠　　幽窓の静坐　緑陰稠し

清晝無人閑可偸　　清昼　人無く　閑偸む可し

一巻詩書心氣爽　　一巻の詩書　心気爽やかに

薫風浄几復何求　　薫風　浄几　復何をか求めん

◆ **大意**　ひっそりした窓のある書斎。静かに坐す。緑の木陰。色濃くなる。清らかな昼。誰もいない。この時間は貴重。詩集一冊。心爽やかに充ち足りる。そよ風と浄机、これ以上なにを求めよう。

◆ **注**　閑可偸＝閑暇を充分楽しもう。几＝机。

梅雨懐郷　五題

Ⅰ （上平・一東）

天昏梅熟紫陽紅　　天昏く　梅は熟し　紫陽紅なり

寂寞茅廬細雨中　　寂寞たる茅廬　細雨の中

一椀新茶促懐舊　　一椀の新茶　懐旧を促す

故山亦恐景濛濛　　故山も亦恐らくは　景濛濛たらん

漢詩のほそみち──春・夏・秋・冬──

◆**大意**　空模様は暗い。梅が熟れ、紫陽花が紅く咲く。もの寂しい隠者の住む茅屋。細かい雨が降る。新茶一杯口に含むと懐旧の情にかられる。故郷も多分、濛濛と雨に煙ぶっていよう。

◆**注**　昏＝くらい。紫陽＝紫陽花。茅廬＝隠者の家。懐舊＝往時を思い出す。

Ⅱ（下平・十二侵）

紫陽花発半晴陰　　紫陽花発けば　晴陰半ばす

午下風來夏未深　　午下風来たるも　夏未だ深からず

千里故山朋友信　　千里の故山　朋友の信

凭窓日暮寂寥心　　窓に凭る日暮　寂寥の心

◆**大意**　紫陽花咲く季節は晴れたり曇つたりする。昼下がりの風。夏は未だ深くない。遠い故郷の友人からの便り。夕暮、窓辺に倚り遥かな故郷を偲べば、湧きでる寂寥の心。

第3部

Ⅲ　（上平・一東）

枇杷黄熟柘榴紅　　枇杷　黄熟し　柘榴紅なり

夢裡故山回想中　　夢裡の故山　回想の中

午搨風來梁燕静　　午搨　風来たり　梁燕静かなり
　　　　　　　　　　　　　　　　　りょうえん

獨愛日暮夕陽穹　　独り愛す　日暮　夕陽の穹

　◆大意　枇杷が熟れ柘榴も紅色になってきた。故郷の山が懐
　　かしい。昼下がり、寛げる椅子に腰掛ける。訪れる風。燕
　　は軒先きの巣でひっそりしている。独りで夕陽の輝く穹を
　　　のきさ　　ねぐら
　　見ていると、己れが本当に愛おしくなる。

　◆注　梁＝屋の棟を支える大きな横木。
　　　　りょう　おく　むね

Ⅳ　（下平・十二侵）

連陰窓暗濕衣襟　　連陰　窓は暗く　衣襟湿す
　　　　　　　　　　　　　　　　　うるお

燕子銜泥午景深　　燕子　泥を銜え　午景深し

千里故山懷往事　　千里の故山　往事を懐う

模糊日暮寂寥心　　模糊たり　日暮　寂寥の心

◆**大意**　連日の雨。窓は暗い。身に付けている服も湿っぽい。泥を銜えた燕が塒に戻る。昼下がりの余韻ある光景。遠い故郷。往事が懐かしい。景色も霞む日暮れ時。物寂しさは望郷の念と重なる。

◆**注**　陰＝しめる、湿り。

V　（下平・十二侵）

新秋細雨畫沈沈	新秋　細雨　昼沈々
水漲天昏夏未深	水漲り　天昏く　夏未だ深からず
閤閤群蛙故山夢	閤々たる群蛙　故山の夢
落梅簷溜寂寥心	落梅　簷溜　寂寥の心

◆**大意**　植えたばかりの田んぼの苗に細い雨が降り続く。昼は静かで深い。水は漲り、天は暗く、夏はまだ深くない。蛙のかまびすしく鳴く光景は、故郷を思い出させる。梅の実が落ち、軒下の雨だれも物寂しい。

◆**注**　新秋＝植えたばかりの苗。沈沈＝深いこと。簷溜＝軒の雨だれ。

第3部

梅天閑詠　三題

Ⅰ（上平・一東）

梅霖連日一陽空　　梅霖　連日　一陽も空し

滿地青苔濕潤中　　地に満つ　青苔　濕潤の中

閑見軒頭梅子落　　閑に見る　軒頭　梅子落つ

小斎煎茗興何窮　　小斎　茗を煎れば　興何ぞ窮まらんや

　◆**大意**　連日の雨。陽は出ない。庭一杯に青い苔。じめじめ
　　している。ふと軒先を見ると梅の実の落ちる気配。書斎で
　　茶を淹れると心が限りなく高まり、楽しくなる。

　◆**注**　霖＝三日以上降りつづく雨。茗＝茶。

Ⅱ（下平・十二侵）

梅霖連日鬱陶心　　梅霖　連日　鬱陶の心

小院階前青蘚侵　　小院の階前　青蘚侵す

獨坐煎茶排悶處　　独坐し茶を煎る　悶を排する処

古藤引蔓緑陰深　　古藤　蔓を引き　緑陰深し

150

漢詩のほそみち──春・夏・秋・冬──

◆**大意**　連日の雨は鬱陶しい。我が家の階段の下の石畳みには青い苔が広がっている。独り坐し茶を淹れるのもいい。厭なことを忘れる。藤の古びた蔓が長く伸び、緑が色濃くなっている。

◆**注**　青蘚＝青い苔（こけ）。悶（もん）＝もだえること。

Ⅲ　（上平・一東）

蕭然細雨緑陰濛	蕭然たる細雨　緑陰濛たり
連日天昏南牖中	連日　天昏く　南牖（なんゆう）の中
獨坐煎茶凝黙想	独坐し　茶を煎て　黙想を凝らす
殘花委地度斜風	残花　地に委し　斜風度（わた）る

◆**大意**　寂しげに細い雨が降る。緑陰は濛としている。南に面する窓から見える空模様は暗い。独り茶を淹れて坐し、ひたすら黙想を凝らす。残っていた花たちはみな大地に散り落ち、風が斜めに吹きつけている。

◆**注**　蕭然＝ものさびしいすがた。牖（ゆう）＝窓。

151

第3部

梅天小酌　二題

Ⅰ (上平・一東)

梅天漠漠一望空　　梅天　漠々　一望空し

黙坐自憐田舎翁　　黙坐し　自ら憐れむ　田舎の翁

酌酒懷人閑日午　　酒を酌めば　人を懷う　閑日午

籬邊三兩紫陽紅　　籬辺　三両　紫陽紅なり

◆**大意**　梅雨空は漠々として見通しがきかない。黙坐し、自
　らを田舎の爺いと憐れむばかり。酒を酌むと人恋しくなる。
　閑日の昼下がり。まがきの辺り、紫陽花が二三の紅花を咲
　かせている。

Ⅱ (下平・十二侵)

浹旬細雨濕衣襟　　浹旬の細雨　衣襟を湿す

檐滴蕭蕭一曲琴　　檐滴　蕭々　一曲の琴

隱几懷朋梅子落　　几に倚り　朋を懷へば　梅子落つ

把杯欲遣寂寥心　　杯を把り遣らんと欲す　寂寥の心

漢詩のほそみち──春・夏・秋・冬──

◆**大意** 細い雨が十日も降りつづけている。衣服は湿ってしまった。軒から滴り落ちる雨だれの音は物さびしく一曲の琴の調べ。机に倚りかかって友を想う。梅の実が落ちる気配。遣りきれない侘びしさ。酒でも酌んで寂寥の心を慰めよう。

◆**注** 浹旬（きょうじゅん）＝一〇日に亘る。蕭々（しょうしょう）＝もの寂しいさま。隠る（よる）＝倚る。

梅天即事（上平・八齊）

禾田環屋燕飛低	禾田（かでん）　屋を環り（めぐり）　燕飛ぶ低し
閣閣鳴蛙東又西	閣々たる　鳴蛙（めいあ）　東又西
細雨晴邊村路滑	細雨晴れる辺り　村路滑らかなり
薫風初動寄新題	薫風　初めて動き　新題を寄す

◆**大意** 田んぼが家の周囲を取り巻き、燕が低く飛んでいる。蛙の大合唱があちらこちらに聞こえる。細い雨の晴れている辺りに、滑らかな村の小路が見える。薫風がようようそよぎ始める。新しい題の詩を歌うことにしよう。

◆**注** 禾田＝水田。

153

第3部

消夏雑詠　四題

Ⅰ　（下平・八庚）

山居六月葛衣輕	山居　六月　葛衣軽し
一望清陰涼意盈	一望の清陰　涼意盈つ
遮断紅塵人不到	紅塵を遮断し　人到らず
潺湲洗耳石泉聲	潺湲　耳を洗う　石泉の声

◆**大意**　夏の山荘。軽い葛織の衣装。涼しい清らかな陰。世
塵を離れ訪問客もいない。泉の音の清々しさが心地よい。

◆**注**　葛衣＝葛織の布製の衣。紅塵＝俗世間。潺湲＝水の流
れるさま。

Ⅱ　（下平・七陽）

松風謖謖坐僧房	松風　謖々　僧房に坐す
泉韻潺潺侵草堂	泉韻　潺々　草堂を侵す
縷縷茶煙閑白晝	縷々たる茶煙　白昼閑たり
山中清爽世塵忘	山中の清爽　世塵を忘る

◆**大意**　松風が吹く。わたくしは禅の修行に相応しいような部屋にひっそり坐している。泉の湧く韻律が、渓流の流れと調和してきこえる。茶煙の立ち昇る光景。昼間の静けさ。清く爽やかな山荘。塵の世を忘れさせる。

◆**注**　謖謖（しょくしょく）＝松風の声。潺潺（せんせん）＝浅い渓流の流れるさま、その声。縷縷（るる）＝細く絶え間のないさま。

Ⅲ（下平・七陽）

欲忘三伏坐僧房	三伏を忘れんと欲し　僧房に坐す
六尺湘簾晝自涼	六尺の湘簾　昼自ずから涼し
竹影當窓風籟爽	竹影　窓に当たり　風籟爽やかに
茶煙昇處白雲郷	茶煙　昇る処　白雲の郷

◆**大意**　酷暑を忘れようと僧房に坐す。六尺の簾の下がる部屋は昼も涼しい。竹影が窓に当たり、風の音も爽やか。茶煙の上がる今いる処は正に隠者の住む別世界である。

◆**注**　伏＝陰暦六月の節の名。夏至の後の第三庚を初伏、第四庚を中伏、立秋後の初庚を末伏と称し、三伏＝酷暑。僧房＝本来、僧侶のいる部屋。白雲郷＝隠者の住む世界。

第3部

Ⅳ （下平・一先）

炎蒸三伏火雲天　　炎蒸　三伏　火雲の天
時醒黒甜涼乱蟬　　時に黒甜を醒まし　乱蟬涼し
縷縷茶煙将忘夏　　縷々たる茶煙　将に夏を忘れんとす
午風扇暑夕陽前　　午風　暑を扇ぐ　夕陽の前

◆**大意**　蒸されるような酷暑。炎のように燃えている雲。時に昼寝を眼醒まさせる蟬の乱れ鳴きは、たまゆらの涼しさを喚起させ、立ち昇る茶煙は夏の暑さを忘れさせる。昼下がりの風は暑さを扇ぐ。夕陽の訪れる前である。

◆**注**　黒甜〔こくてん〕＝昼寝。

暑伏雑詠　（下平・一先）

炎氛焦土夏深天　　炎氛〔えんふん〕　土を焦がす　夏深き天
溽暑解衣流汗偏　　溽暑　衣を解くも　流汗偏〔ひとえ〕なり
竹氣吹香茶可煮　　竹気　香を吹き　茶煮る可し
颯然風起北窓前　　颯然　風起こる　北窓の前

漢詩のほそみち──春・夏・秋・冬──

◆**大意**　炎の妖気が大地を焦がす。夏の深い天空。酷い暑さ。
衣の紐を緩めても汗は吹き出してくる。竹の香が暑さを和
ませる。茶を淹れよう。北窓辺りに風が吹き起こる気配が
ある。

◆**注**　炎氛＝もえあがる（炎）、悪い気（氛）。偏＝かたよって。

暑日読書　二題

I（下平・七陽）

炎陽燋石正煌煌	炎陽　石を焦がし　正に煌々
裸袒嚼氷居草堂	裸袒　氷を嚼み　草堂に居す
永晝拈詩欲忘暑	永昼詩を拈し　暑を忘れんと欲す
獨愉閑適漏聲長	独り閑適を愉しみ　漏声長し

◆**大意**　煌々と陽が照りつけ石を焦がしている。肌脱ぎ姿。
氷を口に含み、静かな草堂にいる。昼は長い。暑さを忘れ
るには詩を拈るに限る。閑を愉み独り口誦む。詩創作の用
語のあれこれ。

◆**注**　燋がす＝焦がす。裸袒＝衣を解き肩を現すこと。拈＝
ひねる。漏声＝詩語あれこれを声に漏らす。

157

第3部

Ⅱ　（下平・一先）

短床裸袒北窓前	短床　裸袒　北窓の前
忘暑讀書思入玄	暑を忘れ　読書　思い玄に入る
風竹珊珊還我處	風竹　珊々　我に還る処
射眸返照噪殘蟬	眸を射る　返照　残蝉噪ぐ

◆**大意**　板張りの床。肌脱ぎ姿。北窓の部屋。暑を忘れ読書三昧、思いは微妙に深遠な境地に入る。竹の笹が鳴り、我に還る。ふと眼を上げる。夕陽が眩しい。蝉が騒がしい。

◆**注**　短床＝板張りのささやかな場所。玄＝微妙に奥深い境地。珊珊＝竹笹の風に鳴る音。返照＝夕陽の輝き。

崖下汲泉　（下平・七陽）

一山深樹色蒼蒼	一山の深樹　色蒼々たり
溪韻淙淙聊促涼	渓韻　淙々　聊か涼を促す
崖下清泉似氷冷	崖下の清泉　氷に似て冷ややかなり
掌中一掬暑何妨	掌中一掬　暑何ぞ妨げんや

漢詩のほそみち――春・夏・秋・冬――

◆**大意**　青あおと茂る深山の樹木。渓流音はさらさら。静けさを深め、涼しさが増す。崖下の泉。氷の冷たさ。掌に掬い口に含むと、如何なる暑さにも耐えられよう。

◆**注**　淙淙＝水の流れるさま、その声。似る＝「如く」の意。

水亭夏花 （下平・一先）

捲簾水榭小池邊	簾を捲く水榭　小池の辺り
獨領清風花影鮮	独り清風を領し　花影鮮やかなり
似玉芙容初綻處	玉に似たり　芙容　初めて綻ぶ処
波心欲語暗香傳	波心　語らんと欲し　暗香伝う

◆**大意**　簾を捲くあずまやのある池の辺。清風の独り占め。鮮やかな影は玉に似た花を綻ばせる芙蓉。漣立つ池の水心。何か語ろうとして秘めた香が漂ってくる。

◆**注**　榭＝屋のある台。うてな。波心＝波の真ん中。水心。

159

第3部

夏雨雑詠 （上平・十灰）

遙雷殷殷黒雲陪　　遥雷　殷々　黒雲陪^{はい}し

倏忽閃光催雨來　　倏忽^{しゅくこつ}　閃光　雨を催して来たる

簷滴躍珠炎暑去　　簷滴　珠を躍らせ　炎暑去る

長虹一幅壓浮埃　　長虹一幅　浮埃^{ふあい}を圧す

◆**大意**　遥雷の音いんいん。黒雲が加わる。忽ち閃く光。降
り注ぐ雨。軒下に滴る玉のような雨。炎暑は去る。虹がで
る。大きい。浮き漂うほこりを鎮め暑さは忽ち去る。

◆**注**　殷殷＝音の盛んなさま。陪^{はい}＝加わる。満ちる。重なる。
伴う。倏^{しゅく}＝忽ち、速やか。浮埃＝軽いほこり。

暑伏雑詠 （上平・一東）

夏深難耐暑如烘　　夏深く　耐え難し　暑烘^やくが如し

流汗披襟午睡空　　流汗　襟を披^{ひら}けど　午睡空し

六尺湘簾茶可煮　　六尺の湘簾　茶煮る可し

颯然風起響丁東　　颯然　風起こり　響き丁東^{とうとう}

漢詩のほそみち──春・夏・秋・冬──

◆**大意**　夏が深い。耐え難い暑さ。焼かれるようだ。流れる汗。襟を抜いても眠れない。簾のある部屋で茶でも淹れよう。すると風湧き起こり、風鈴の音。チリンチリン。

◆**注**　烘＝火を焚く、燃やす。丁東＝タウトウ、テイトウ。風鈴などの触れあう声。

白雨送涼（下平・一先）

夏深草緑日如年　　夏深く　草緑に　日は年の如し

雲黒雷聲六月天　　雲は黒く　雷声　六月の天

白雨沛然風颯颯　　白雨　沛然として　風颯々たり

清涼忽起滿襟邊　　清涼　忽ち起こり　襟辺に満つ

◆**大意**　夏が深い。緑の草が豊か。日は年のように長い。黒雲が湧き、雷が轟く真夏の空模様。激しいにわか雨の後、気持ち良い風が吹く。涼が訪れ、襟の辺りが爽やかになる。

◆**注**　白雨＝俄か雨。沛然＝雨の盛んに降るさま。

161

第3部

驟雨　二題

Ⅰ（上平・十灰）

雲奔風起聴遙雷　　　雲奔り　風起こり　遥雷を聴く

閃閃電光從雨來　　　閃々たる電光　雨を従えて来る

天地蘇生簷雨急　　　天地　蘇生し　簷雨急なり

早秋涼到洗浮埃　　　早秋　涼は到るか　浮埃を洗う

◆**大意**　雲激しく動き、風起こり、遠雷を聞く。稲光閃き、雨となる。天地甦り、軒から雨滴が激しく滴り落ちる。すると一抹の涼が秋の気配を齎す。暑熱を溜めた塵埃を綺麗に洗ってくれる驟雨。

◆**注**　奔る＝「走る」より更に勢いがいい。

Ⅱ（上平・十灰）

油然雲漲聴遙雷　　　油然　雲は漲り　遥雷を聴く

電影狂奔氣快哉　　　電影　狂奔し　気快なる哉

驟雨滂沱蘇萬物　　　驟雨　滂沱　万物を蘇らす

涼風颯颯入窓來　　　涼風　颯々　窓に入り来る

漢詩のほそみち──春・夏・秋・冬──

◆**大意**　雲が湧き起こり、遠雷を聞く。稲妻が激しく閃き、気分は爽快。激しい雨が降り、萬物は蘇生する。窓から入る涼風。この爽やかさ。

◆**注**　油然(ゆうぜん)＝雲の起こるさま。滂沱(ほうだ)＝雨の盛んに降るさま。

渓頭垂釣（下平・七陽）

夏深曳杖白雲郷　　夏深く　杖を曳く　白雲の郷

垂釣渓頭晝尚涼　　釣を渓頭に垂るれば　昼尚涼し

流水潺潺竿不動　　流水　潺々(せんせん)　竿(かん)動かず

魚籃空處已斜陽　　魚籃(ぎょらん)　空しき処　已に斜陽

◆**大意**　夏が深い。杖を曳き、わたくしは白雲棚引く隠者の里を散歩する。谷川の辺に釣り糸を垂れると、昼も涼しい。水は潺潺と流れ、竿は動かない。獲った魚を入れる筈の魚籠は空っぽ。陽はすでに西に傾いている。

◆**注**　白雲郷＝隠者の住む處に白雲は棚引く。魚籃(ぎょらん)＝魚を入れる籠。

第3部

第三章　秋

初秋偶成　四題

I （上平・四支）

蟬聲切切立秋時	蝉声　切々　立秋の時
日暮涼生節序移	日暮　涼生じ　節序移る
露滴梧桐蟲韻起	露は梧桐に滴り　虫韻起こり
風檐獨坐賦新詩	風檐（ふうえん）　独り坐し　新詩を賦す

◆**大意**　蝉がしきりに鳴いている。秋の訪れを感じさせる。日暮れどきは涼しい。季節の移ろい。早々と夜露は梧桐に滴り、虫が鳴く。風の吹き通う軒場（のき）に独り坐し、詩を一つ作る。

◆**注**　節序＝時節の移る次第。風檐＝風の吹きかよう軒場。

164

漢詩のほそみち──春・夏・秋・冬──

Ⅱ （上平・六魚）

梧桐搖落報秋初　　梧桐　揺落　秋を報じる初め

籬畔蟲聲野叟居　　籬畔の虫声　野叟の居

叢草露零殘暑退　　叢草　露零ち　残暑退く

涼風窗下欲繙書　　涼風の窓下　書を繙かんと欲す

◆**大意**　桐の葉が揺れ落ち、秋の訪れを知る。まがきに虫の鳴き声のする野人の住居。草むらに滴る夜露。残暑も薄らいでくる。この涼風の通う窓辺で書を繙こう。

◆**注**　零ち＝滴る。野叟＝野人。叟は老人、おきなの意。

Ⅲ （下平・六麻）

紫薇花艶夕陽斜　　紫薇花艶にして　夕陽斜めなり

樹上殘蟬愁緒加　　樹上の残蝉　愁緒加わる

日挂西山欺畫筆　　日は西山に挂り　画筆を欺く

秋宵氣爽興無涯　　秋宵　気は爽やかにして興涯りなし

第3部

◆**大意** 艶のあるさるすべりの花に夕陽がさしている。その
つるんとした樹皮に蝉が止まり鳴くのは、詩的哀感さえ湧
く。夕陽が西山の端に沈もうとしている光景は、筆舌に尽
しがたい。暮れていく秋の爽やかさ。限りなく興が湧く。

Ⅳ （下平・八庚）

西風颯颯趁秋晴	西風　颯々　秋晴を趁う
來往白雲筇履輕	来往する白雲　筇履軽し
恰促吟情梧葉落	恰も吟情を促し　梧葉落つ
蟲鳴還援一詩成	虫鳴き　還た援け　一詩成る

◆**大意** 西風そよぐ秋晴れに誘われて野にでる。ゆききする
白い雲。杖を曳くこの身は軽やか。桐の葉が落ちる。詩情
をそそる。虫の鳴き声も歌ごころを促してくれる。こうし
て詩ができた。

◆**注** 趁う＝追う。来往＝ゆきき、往来。筇＝杖。吟情＝詩
人の歌ごころ。

漢詩のほそみち──春・夏・秋・冬──

新秋野興 （下平・十一尤）

澄天片片白雲浮	澄天　片々　白雲浮かぶ
小院胡枝花影稠	小院の胡枝　花影稠し
滿地蟲聲風露冷	滿地の虫声　風露冷ややかに
新秋野興詩可酬	新秋の野興　詩もて酬ゆべし

◆**大意**　天は澄み白雲が浮かぶ。我が庭の萩の花枝。影を揺
らせて愛おしい。大地いちめん虫の声。しっとり、夜露と
風。新秋の野趣。よし、詩にうたおう。

◆**注**　胡枝＝萩。風露（ふうろ）＝風と露。

秋日郊行　三題

I （下平・八庚）

西郊徑盡遠山横	西郊　径尽きて　遠山横わる
秋色尋來杖履輕	秋色　尋ね来れば　杖履軽し
紅白胡枝殘照裡	紅白の胡枝　残照の裡
村巷暮早一燈明	村巷　暮るること早く　一燈明らかなり

第3部

◆**大意** 秋の野辺。小径の盡きるところ、彼方に遠山がみえ
る。秋を求めるわたくしの杖も足もかるい。紅白の萩の花
を夕陽が照らしだす。とある家の窓からは灯りが漏れる。
村里は暮れるのが早い。

◆**注** 西郊＝秋の野辺。

Ⅱ （下平・六麻）

西郊幽徑夕陽斜	西郊の幽径　夕陽斜めなり
村女籬邊採菊花	村女　籬辺（りへん）　菊花を採る
籠裡清香滿衣袂	籠裡の清香　衣袂（いべい）に満つ
一窓燈火野人家	一窓の灯火　野人の家

◆**大意** 秋。野辺の小径を夕陽が斜めに照らし、村の娘が籬
辺の菊花を採っている。手に持つ籠からは漂う菊の清香。
彼女の衣いっぱいに広がっている。一窓に灯火。飾らない
土地の人の家。

◆**注** 衣袂（いべい）（ころも）＝衣。袂＝たもと。

168

漢詩のほそみち──春・夏・秋・冬──

Ⅲ （下平・七陽）

蜻蜓緩緩帯斜陽	蜻蜓　緩々として　斜陽を帯ぶ
畦畔稲花生郁香	畦畔の稲花　郁香を生ず
秋到郊墟風欲白	秋は郊墟に到り　風白からんと欲す
新涼一夕暮山蒼	新涼　一夕　暮山蒼し

◆**大意**　夕陽のなか蜻蛉がのんびり飛んでいる。畦道からは花を付けた稲穂の香が漂う。郊外に訪れた秋、吹く風も秋めく。新涼の今宵、暮れ行く山々の蒼さも愛おしい。

◆**注**　蜻蜓＝蜻蜓洲（日本国）＝蜻蛉。緩緩＝ゆるやかなさま。

秋夜吟 （下平・八庚）

西風蕭颯早寒生	西風　蕭颯　早寒生ず
獨坐孤燈夜未更	独坐　孤灯　夜未だ更けず
庭院啾啾蟲語急	庭院　啾々　虫語急なり
十三夜月讀書情	十三夜月　読書の情

第3部

◆**大意** 西風がさびしそうに吹き、少々寒さも加わる。灯火の下、独り坐す。まだ夜は更けていない。庭には虫たちが今を限りに秋を歌っている。今宵は十三夜月。ひたすら読書欲に駆られる。

◆**注** 蕭^{しょう}＝もの寂しいの意。颯＝風の吹く音（颯々）。啾啾＝虫や鳥が小声で鳴くこと。

江村秋興 （下平・七陽）

江村小徑弄秋光	江村の小径　秋光を弄す
雞犬無聲萬頃涼	鶏犬　声無く　万頃涼なり
樹梢殘蟬風颯颯	樹梢の残蝉　風颯々たり
晴空一碧稻花香	晴空　一碧　稲花香し

◆**大意** 川辺の村里の小径に秋の光が戯れ、鶏は鳴かず犬も吠えない。広い水田に秋涼が忍びこむ。樹梢の残蝉は秋風に晒されている。晴れ渡る碧^{あお}い空。稲の花が芳しく薫る。

◆**注** 江村^{こうそん}＝川に沿うむら。狛江は多摩川に沿う。雞犬＝にわとりと犬（村邑の家畜、邑＝むらさと）。頃^{けい}＝水田百畝をいう。

漢詩のほそみち――春・夏・秋・冬――

秋夜對月　三題

I　（上平・十四寒）

窓前風竹玉珊珊	窓前の風竹　玉珊々
墜露無聲坐夜闌	墜露　声無く　夜闌に坐す
皓皓月光人盡望	皓々たる月光　人尽く望む
桂花郁郁一燈寒	桂花　郁々　一灯寒し

◆**大意**　窓前の茂る竹の葉に玉露が光る。露は音もなく滴り
　落ち、更けていく夜陰にわたくしは唯ひとり坐している。
　冴えて美しいこの月を、人々は皆愛でているだろう。金木
　犀の花が薫り、灯火は寂しく愛おしい。

◆**注**　珊珊＝露の光るさま。闌＝たけなわ。皓皓＝月の光の
　明るいさま。郁郁＝香氣の盛んなさま。寒し＝寂しい。

第 3 部

Ⅱ　（下平・十一尤）

西風颯颯正中秋　　　西風　颯々　正に中秋

叢裡蟲聲白露幽　　　叢裡の虫声　白露幽なり

今夜十三明月影　　　今夜十三　明月の影

迎君置酒醉南樓　　　君を迎え　置酒し　南楼に酔わん

◆**大意**　西風が吹く。正に中秋。草むらに鳴く虫の声。夜露
　　が微かに光る。今宵は十三夜の明月。酒を用意し、きみを
　　迎え、南面の高楼（書斎）で酔いしれよう。

Ⅲ　（下平・十一尤）

西風吹老暮雲収　　　西風　吹き老い　暮雲収まる

院落露華桂氣幽　　　院落　露華　桂気幽なり

如畫東天明月夜　　　昼の如く　東天　明月の夜

些知詩酒蔑王侯　　　些か知る　詩酒　王侯を蔑んずるを

◆**大意**　西風も秋色を深めている。夕暮れの雲も消えた。垣
　　根内の座敷は夜露に囲まれ、金木犀の香りが幽かに匂う。

昼のように明るい東の天。明月の証である。このような良
宵に飲む酒は、王侯貴族に勝ると知る。

◆注　院＝道士・学者の居所。院落＝垣根で囲む座敷。蘇軾
詩＝歌菅楼台声寂寂／鞦韆院落夜沈沈（「春宵一刻値千金」
参照。些か＝いささか（些細）。

秋夜閑詠（下平・十一尤）

桂香粉散月光幽	桂花　粉として散じ　月光幽なり
風韻蕭蕭顥氣流	風韻　蕭々　顥気流る
故友魚書懷往事	故友の魚書　往事を懐う
凭窗獨坐奈郷愁	窓に凭り独り坐せば　郷愁を奈せん

◆大意　金木犀の花香が粉のように飛び散り、月光が幽やか
に辺りを照らしだしている。風の調べはもの寂しく、天辺
には白く明るい気が流れている。旧友からきたしみの付い
た昔の手紙を読みなおしていると、往事がなつかしい。窓
に凭りかかり独り坐していると、湧いてくる郷愁をどうす
ることもできない。

◆注　顥気＝天辺の白く明らかなる気。故友＝友人。魚＝染
み。魚書＝しみの付いた古い手紙。

173

第3部

桂花　三題

Ⅰ（下平・八庚）

月光皓皓桂花榮　　月光　皓々として　桂花栄え

金粟相連色益明　　金粟相連なり　色 益ます 明らかなり

馥郁芳香風細細　　馥郁たる　芳香　風細々

吟心自動一窓清　　吟心　自ずから動き　一窓清し

- ◆ **大意**　皓々と月は輝き、金木犀の花もいまを盛りに咲き誇
  っている。金色のあわ粒のような花また花。その色が月光
  に冴える。馥郁と漂う独特の香。微かに風が吹く。歌心が
  自然に湧きおこり、書斎の窓も清らかに輝いている。

- ◆ **注**　粟（しょく、そく、ぞく）＝あわ粒。金粟＝桂花。

Ⅱ（上平・十四寒）

秋心欲賦倚欄干　　秋心　賦さんと欲し　欄干に倚る

一簇桂花今正闌　　一簇の桂花　今正に闌たけなわなり

金粟映陽看不盡　　金粟陽に映じて　看れども尽きず

芬芳馥郁透詩肝　　芬芳ふんほう　馥郁　詩肝に透る

漢詩のほそみち──春・夏・秋・冬──

◆**大意**　秋の心を詩に歌おうと思い、欄干に寄り掛かる。一
　簇の桂花が今、真っ盛りである。金いろのあわ粒状の花が
　陽の光を浴びて見飽きない。えも言えない高貴な香が詩魂
　に浸透していく。

◆**注**　芬芳＝香りのよいこと。書經「治之至者、芬芳香気動
　於神明」。詩肝＝詩心（うたごころ）。

Ⅲ（下平・八庚）

桂花香處露晶晶　　　桂花　香る処　露晶々

今夕金葩浸月明　　　今夕　金葩　月明に浸る

騒客不眠秋漾漾　　　騒客　眠らず　秋漾々たり

一詩未就到深更　　　一詩　未だ就らず　深更に到る

◆**大意**　金木犀の花薫る処、露も煌めき光っている。今宵、
　その金色の花は月明りに濡れている。静かで清らかな秋の
　夜。わたくしは眠れないでいる。詩は未だできていない。
　夜は更けていく。

◆**注**　晶晶＝煌めき光るさま。葩＝はな（華）、丹葩など。

第 3 部

山寺観楓　三題

I （下平・十二侵）

秋容山寺夕陽深	秋容の山寺　夕陽深し
恰是仙郷楓樹林	恰も是れ仙郷　楓樹の林
霜葉映紅眞似畫	霜葉　紅に映じ　真に画に似たり
晩鐘隠隠促吟心	晩鐘　隠々として　吟心を促す

◆**大意**　秋の山寺に夕陽が輝く。その光景はまるで楓の林に囲まれた仙郷さながら。霜に打たれた葉も紅に染まり、まるで絵そのもの。微かに聞こえる夕暮れの鐘声。歌ごころを掻きたてる。

◆**注**　容＝かたち、すがた。隠隠＝微かにして明らかならざるさま。

漢詩のほそみち──春・夏・秋・冬──

Ⅱ （上平・一東）

探秋青女夕陽中	秋を探れば　青女　夕陽の中
楓樹将然錦繡工	楓樹将に然えんとし　錦繡工なり
山寺映紅眞似畫	山寺　紅に映じ　真に画に似たり
吟筇林徑興無窮	吟筇　林径　興窮まり無し

◆**大意**　秋を探る。夕陽のなかに秋の女神が輝いている。楓の紅色は真っ盛り。巧みな錦の刺繡さながら。彼方の山寺も紅に映えて一幅の絵。筇を曳く林の小径。興味津しん。

◆**注**　青女＝秋の女神。錦繡＝にしきと、ぬいとりと。工＝優れている。

Ⅲ （上平・一東）

友風繞澗訪禪宮	風を友とし　澗を繞り　禅宮を訪う
四面山腰楓葉紅	四面の山腰　楓葉の紅
青女描秋衣欲染	青女　秋を描き　衣染めんと欲す
吟筇獨植夕陽中	吟筇　独り植てる　夕陽の中

第3部

◆**大意** 風に身を委ね、渓谷の水の流れを追う中にとある禅寺を訪うことになる。楓葉の紅に染められた四方の山々。女神の描く秋の美しさ。筆者の衣も秋の風情に染められて仕舞いそう。夕陽を浴びながらじっくり秋を味わおうと、杖を植てて立ち止まるわたくし。

◆**注** 澗＝たにみず。　植＝筇を植てるは立ち止まること。

晩秋即事　二題

I　（上平・十四寒）

柿枝残子似瓊丹	柿枝の残子　瓊の丹きに似て
霜葉嬋娟不足看	霜葉は嬋娟　看れども足らず
蕭瑟西風秋已老	蕭瑟たる西風　秋已に老ゆ
帰鴉鳴處一天寒	帰鴉　鳴く処　一天寒し

◆**大意** 柿の枝に残る紅く熟れた美しい玉の実。霜に打たれた葉の艶やかな色彩。見飽きない。寂しげな西風の吹くきょう日はすでに秋も老いている。鳴きながら塒に帰る鴉の姿。空もうすら寒い。

◆**注** 瓊（けい、ぎょう）＝美しい玉。丹。嬋娟＝姿の美しく艶やかなさま。蕭瑟＝もの寂しいさま。

漢詩のほそみち──春・夏・秋・冬──

Ⅱ （上平・十三元）

飛楓紅盡寂荒園　　飛楓　紅は尽き　荒園寂たり

裸木霜痕落日昏　　裸木　霜痕　落日昏（くら）し

四壁秋寒人亦老　　四壁　秋寒くして　人亦老ゆ

風聲瑟瑟晚鴉飜　　風声　瑟々　晩鴉飜る

　◆大意　楓の紅葉は散り尽くし、庭は寂寥。裸になった木々
　に霜の痕跡。夕暮れの日差しは昏（くら）い。辺りの寒さは晩秋を
　告げる。わたくしも老いた。寂しく吹く風。鴉も塒に向か
　っている。

晩秋偶成 （上平・十四寒）

西風入樹葉聲乾　　西風 樹に入り　葉声乾く

庭院蕭條蟲語酸　　庭院　蕭条（さん）　虫語酸たり

墜露籬邊秋欲逝　　墜露　籬辺　秋逝かんと欲す

孤燈誰慰思無端　　孤灯 誰か慰めん　思い端（はしな）無きを

第3部

◆**大意**　秋風が樹肌に食い込み、葉の囁きも枯れてきた。庭の風情も寂しげで、虫声に夏の色気がない。まがきの辺りに夜露が滴り、秋も逝こうとしている。孤独な灯火のもと、とりとめもない思いに耽るわたくしを一体、誰が慰めてくれようか。

◆**注**　酸＝いたましい。無端＝はしなき、初めと終りが分からない。端＝かぎり。

送秋偶成（上平・十四寒）

空庭寂寂一天寒	空庭　寂々　一天寒し
今歳已知秋色殘	今歳　已に知る　秋色残すを
瑟瑟風聲霜信早	瑟々たる風声　霜信早し
歸鴉何處喚愁攢	帰鴉何れの処か　愁いを喚んで攢す

◆**大意**　庭の樹も落葉し天は寒々としている。今年も秋の風情が僅かに残る頃となった。風も寂しげで、霜の訪れも早い。塒に帰る鴉が何処かで鳴いている。愁いを喚起し、いつしか群れをなしている。

◆**注**　攢す＝集まること。

漢詩のほそみち――春・夏・秋・冬――

秋夜懷友（下平・十二侵）

籬邊唧唧一燈深	籬辺　唧々（しょくしょく）　一灯深し
萬里鄉関寂寞心	万里　郷関　寂寞の心
喟樹江雲君健否	喟樹江雲　君健なるや否や
吟愁満臆涙沾襟	吟愁　臆（むね）に満ち　涙襟を沾す（うるお）

◆**大意**　籬（まがき）の辺りには虫が寂しそうに鳴き、灯が一つ秋の夜
を際だたせている。郷里を遠く離れた寂寞の心。ふる里の
友は元気にしているだろうか。そう考えると憂いと詩情が
湧き、襟も涙で濡れ（ぬ）てしまう。

◆**注**　唧唧（しょくしょく）＝虫の鳴く声。喟樹江雲（いじゅこううん）＝遠方の友を思う情の切
なさ。杜甫、春日懐李白詩「喟は北に春の天樹、江は東に
日暮の雲」＝暮雲春樹。吟愁＝ため息をつきたくなるよう
な愁いごころ。臆（むね）＝胸。沾（うるおす）。

第3部

鶴賀城跡 （下平・七陽）

暮山人去野花香　　暮山　人去って　野花香し

満目荒涼古戦場　　満目　荒涼　古戦場

憶往獨憐残塁下　　往を憶い　独り憐れむ　残塁の下

蟲聲喞喞促愁腸　　虫声　喞々　愁腸を促す

◆注　暮山＝暮丘。愁腸＝心うれうること。「愁腸正遇断猿時」（劉禹錫詩）

［英訳］

Ruins of Tsuruga Castle

Visitors left the site of our hill's castle for the fragrance of flowers,
Now deserted and bleak is this ancient battlefield.
Thinking about the past, I stand alone on the remains of the citadel,
The voices of insects in fall drive me to the deep contemplation.

漢詩のほそみち──春・夏・秋・冬──

第四章　冬

初冬偶成　五題

Ⅰ　（下平・八庚）

西郊曳杖落楓輕　　西郊　杖を曳けば　落楓軽し

短日探詩不計程　　短日　詩を探り　程を計らず

有味小春和暖徑　　味有り　小春　和暖の径

橙黄橘緑滿吟情　　橙黄橘緑　吟情満つ

◆**大意**　秋の野辺。杖を曳く。軽く舞う楓の落葉。日は短い。詩を求め、あてのない散策。小春日和。味わいがある。黄色い橙。緑色の蜜柑。詩情が溢れる。

◆**注**　西郊＝秋の野辺。五行説は西を秋に配置する。春の野を東郊という。程＝距離。橙黄橘緑＝だいだいが黄色を帯び、蜜柑が緑色を呈する。初冬小春の季節。

183

第3部

Ⅱ（上平・四支）

遠鐘何處夕陽時　　遠鐘　何れの処ぞ　夕陽の時

天外遙望月似眉　　天外　遥かに望む　月眉に似たり

小院楓枯籬菊盛　　小院楓は枯れるも　籬菊は盛んなり

栖鴉不語折殘枝　　栖鴉　語らず　折残の枝

　◆**大意**　遠くから鐘の音。何処だろう。夕陽が輝く。天空の
　　月は眉を引いたよう。庭の楓の葉は散ったが、籬の菊は真
　　っ盛り。楓の折残枝に鴉が止まっている。鳴かない。

Ⅲ（下平・七陽）

三餘擁几坐虛堂　　三余　几を擁し　虚堂に坐す

霜氣森森寒月光　　霜気　森々　月光寒し

一穗青燈耽誦讀　　一穂の青灯　誦読に耽る

無妨寂寞夜方長　　寂寞を妨ぐる無く　夜方に長し

　◆**大意**　夜、机を抱くように誰もいない部屋に坐す。霜気迫
　　り、月光は寒気に冴える。燈火のもと、詩の誦読。辺りの
　　寂寞。愛おしい。秋の夜長。

漢詩のほそみち──春・夏・秋・冬──

◆注　三餘＝読書に最も適当な三つの時。冬（年の余）、夜
　　（日の余）、陰雨（時の余）。ここでは夜。

Ⅳ　（上平・五微）

輕寒愛日落楓飛　　　軽寒　愛日　落楓飛ぶ

林下停筇棲鳥歸　　　林下　筇を停めれば　棲鳥帰る

殘菊經霜餘艶徑　　　残菊　霜を経し　余艶の径

橙黄橘緑映斜暉　　　橙黄橘緑　斜暉に映ず

◆大意　薄ら寒い冬のある日、楓の落ち葉が風に舞う。林下
　　に杖を停めると、林を塒にする鳥が戻ってくる。霜に耐え、
　　艶の余る菊たちの映える小径がつづく。初冬小春の季節が
　　夕陽に映じている。

◆注　愛日＝冬の日（左伝「冬日可愛」）。餘艶＝余りの色艶。

185

第3部

V （上平・五微）

黄昏散策落楓飛　　黄昏　散策　落楓飛ぶ

寒色蕭然紅葉稀　　寒色　蕭然　紅葉稀なり

小至殘陽冬尚淺　　小至の残陽　冬尚浅し

荒蹊案句晩鴉歸　　荒蹊　句を案ずれば　晩鴉帰る

◆**大意**　黄昏どきの散歩。楓の落ち葉が舞う。寒さが寂しく漂い、枝に残る紅葉は少ない。冬至前の夕陽の風情。冬は未だ浅い。草は枯れ、地肌むき出しの径。句を捻る。晩鴉が塒に戻ってくる。

◆**注**　小至＝冬至の前の一日。十一月をいう場合もある。

小春村舎 （上平・五微）

逍遙出郭夕陽微　　逍遥　郭を出づれば　夕陽微なり

秋去孤村寂釣磯　　秋は去り　孤村　釣磯寂たり

輕暖田園冬尚淺　　軽暖の田園　冬尚浅く

晩鐘殷殷且忘歸　　晩鐘　殷々　且らく帰るを忘る

漢詩のほそみち——春・夏・秋・冬——

◆**大意**　漫ろ歩き。郊外にでる。微かな夕陽。秋は去り、釣り人もいない侘びしい村の磯辺。軽い暖の気配もある。辺りの田園の冬は未だ浅い。夕暮れの遠鐘。いんいんと聞こえる。未だ帰りたくない。

◆**注**　郭＝都、城、町の外廻りを囲む土壁。

冬夜読書　二題

I　（上平・十四寒）

月纖燈暗坐更闌　　　月纖く　灯暗く　更闌に坐す

繙巻白屋神自安　　　巻を繙けば　白屋　神自ずから安し

知己相逢古書裏　　　知己　相逢うは　古書の裏

忘寒尚友老來歡　　　寒を忘れ　尚友　老来の歡

◆**大意**　月纖く灯火のもと夜は更けていく。詩書を読めばあばら屋であろうがこころは自ずから落ち着く。気持の通う友に会えるのは古典の中である。こうして寒さを忘れ、古人を友とするのが老いの歓びと知る。

◆**注**　更闌＝夜更け。白屋＝はくおく、貧しい家。尚友＝古人を友とすること。

第3部

Ⅱ （上平・六魚）

寒窓掲燭獨耽書　　寒窓　燭を掲げ　独り書に耽る

辛苦忘來心自舒　　辛苦　忘れ来たり　心自ら舒ぶ

朗朗咿唔誰解我　　朗々たる　咿唔　誰か我を解せん

應知老骨野僧如　　応に知るべし　老骨　野僧如たり

◆**大意**　寒い冬の書斎の窓。燈火のもと独り書をよむ。過去
の辛苦など忘れ、心は何か求める想いで緩やかに弾む。声
だして朗誦する。誰がわたくしを理解できよう。知るがい
いこの老人は野僧さながらであると。

◆**注**　舒＝のぶ、緩やかになる。咿唔＝書を読む声。

寒夜読書　二題

Ⅰ （下平・七陽）

書窓皓皓凜寒光　　書窓　皓々として　寒光凜たり

門戸風敲夜正長　　門戸　風敲き　夜正に長し

繙卷三更人未寢　　卷を繙けば　三更　人未だ寢ねず

孤燈将盡轉凄涼　　孤灯　将に尽きんとし　転た凄涼

漢詩のほそみち──春・夏・秋・冬──

◆**大意**　書斎の窓。凜としてこうこうと輝く燈火。寒い。門
　戸を叩く風の音。夜は長い。深夜、独り書をよむ。燈火は
　今を限りとともりつづける。凄涼とした雰囲気が漂う。

◆**注**　三更＝午後 11 時〜午前 1 時頃まで。

Ⅱ（**下平・十二侵**）

侵肌霜氣夜方深	肌を侵す　霜気　夜方に深し
凭几繙書惜寸陰	几に凭り書を繙き　寸陰を惜しむ
鋭意沈潜猶不倦	鋭意　沈潜　猶倦まず
青燈一穗學生心	青灯一穂　学生の心

◆**大意**　肌を刺す霜の気配。深夜。机に向かい、一瞬を惜し
　み書を繙く。精神を統一し、読みつづける。倦むことはな
　い。清らかな燈火。生涯変わらぬ学生の心。

第3部

至日 三題

Ⅰ （上平・五微）

漏春至日暮烟飛　　春を漏らす　至日　暮烟飛ぶ

小院梅梢送夕暉　　小院の梅梢　夕暉を送る

蓬屋風敲寒夜入　　蓬屋　風は敲き　寒夜に入る

一窓斜月映書幃　　一窓の斜月　書幃を映す

◆**大意**　春の前触れの冬至。棚引く暮烟。庭の梅樹の梢に夕陽が輝く。茅屋を風が敲き、夜に入ると寒くなる。窓から斜めに差し込む月光。書斎のカーテンを映しだす。

◆**注**　蓬屋＝あばら家。寒夜入＝夜になって寒くなる。書幃＝ひとえのとばり、書斎のカーテン。

Ⅱ （上平・四支）

南窓風穏暗香吹　　南窓　風穏やかに　暗香吹く

至日如春陰氣衰　　至日　春の如く　陰気衰う

明旦一陽來復處　　明旦　一陽来復の処

喜看已笑早梅枝　　喜び看る　已に笑う　早梅の枝

漢詩のほそみち——春・夏・秋・冬——

◆**大意**　南面の窓。穏やかな風。梅の暗香が仄かに漂う。冬至の日、陰気は衰え春のよう。明朝は一陽来復、春が訪れるかも知れない。早咲きの梅花が已に綻びているのが喜ばしい。

◆**注**　陰＝陽の對。明旦＝明朝。

Ⅲ　（上平・十灰）

一陽來復暖将回　　　一陽来復し　暖将に回らんとするも

風冷未開庭院梅　　　風冷ややかに　未だ開かず　庭院の梅

短日窓前天欲暮　　　短日の窓前　天暮れんと欲す

爐頭溫酒獨傾杯　　　炉頭　酒を温め　独り杯を傾く

◆**大意**　一陽来復。春は近い。だが風は冷たく、庭の梅はまだ開かない。日は短い。早や天は暮れようとしている。居間で酒を温め、独り杯を傾ける。

第3部

除夕祭詩　二題

I （上平・十四寒）

窮陰将逝一氈寒　　窮陰　将に逝かんとし　一氈寒し

落托方知愧自安　　落托　方に知る　自らに安きを愧ず

欲倣浪仙除夕事　　倣わんと欲す浪仙　除夕の事

絶無佳句作詩難　　絶えて佳句無し　作詩は難し

◆**大意**　歳も暮れようとして、毛織り布団でさえ肌寒い。晩年、これ程もの寂しい姿晒すのは刻苦精励しなかったから。おおみそかの夜には唐の詩人・浪仙の故事を見習うがいい。努力の足りないわたくしに佳句はない。作詩は容易でない。

◆**注**　窮陰＝冬の末。氈＝毛織の布団。落托＝もの寂しい、落ちぶれる。浪仙賈島 (780?–843) ＝字は浪仙、唐・范陽の人。初め僧となり、無本と号するが詩才ゆえに韓愈に抜擢され、還俗し長江の主簿となる。賈長江ともいう。「十年磨一剣」（賈島「剣客」詩）はよく知られている。除夕＝おおみそかの夜。

192

漢詩のほそみち──春・夏・秋・冬──

Ⅱ（上平・十四寒）

光陰如矢歳将残　　光陰矢の如く　歳将に残せんとす

落托生涯辛又酸　　落托の生涯　辛また酸

濁酒今宵緩強覓　　濁酒　今宵　緩（かん）強いて覓（もと）む

苦吟一歳祭詩難　　苦吟　一歳　詩を祭ること難し

◆**大意**　光陰は矢の如く、今年もはや盡きようとしている。落ちぶれたわたくしの人生は辛酸の極み。今宵は酒を飲んで緊張感を解きほぐしたい。この一年の艱難辛苦。満足できる詩の創作は難しい。

◆**注**　残す＝盡（ざん）きる。辛また酸＝つらいこと。

除夜偶成（上平・四支）

光陰如矢歳云移　　光陰　矢の如く　歳云（ここ）に移る

志業無成悔已遅　　志業成る無く　悔いるも已に遅し

百八鐘聲双涙滴　　百八の鐘声　双涙滴（したた）り

凄然老懐有誰知　　凄然たる老懐　誰ありてか知らん

◆**大意**　光陰矢の如く今年も暮れようとしている。志を遂げることなく、今更後悔しても時すでに遅しである。除夜の鐘をきいていると涙が滴り落ちる。寂しく痛ましい老いの身の想い。誰がこの惨めな気持ちを分かってくれるだろうか。

◆**注**　凄（せい）＝寒い、さびしい、痛ましい。凄然＝寒く痛ましい。

あとがき

　第一部は『アレーティア』29号に掲載済み。筆者は魂の成長を求めて止まないEndymionと自らを重ねたい。神話と現実の重層（cf.写真）は全体に影を落とす。第二部は三章に分かれ、微かに華やぐ日常生活における過去現在の断片的描写である。第三部「漢詩のほそみち――春夏秋冬」は、老いの侘びしさを四季の移ろいに反映させている。漢詩は、通信添削における修正の少ない作品を中心に試行錯誤の習作群。拝眉の榮に恵まれない幻の師の許可はない。忸怩たる思いが残る。

　使用文献『誰にもできる漢詩の作り方』太刀掛呂山(1988)、『詩語集成』川田瑞穂（松雲堂書店・復刻版2000）他。

　顧みると、遅遅とした己の心の歩みが恨めしい。何れにせよ、拙さを顧みず『遥かなる旅路――キーツ・エッセイ・漢詩』と題し、躊躇逡巡の末、私家版上梓に思い到った。知的好奇心の記録は残したい。卒寿は近い。

　本書は旧漢字の多い漢詩の横書きを含め、音羽書房鶴見書店社長・山口隆史氏のご好意に負うところが大きい。衷心より感謝の意を表したい。

2017年8月吉日

　　　　　　　　　　　　　　　　　　髙橋　雄四郎

著者略歴

髙橋　雄四郎（たかはし　ゆうしろう）

1927 年生まれ。戸次尋常小学校、大分中学校卒業。敗戦後、農業の
傍ら大分経済専門学校卒業。津久見高等学校教諭を経て上京。早稲
田大学文学部、英文学専修第 3 学年に編入学。早稲田大学大学院進
学、単位取得。Cambridge に於ける研究生活を経て、実践女子大学
名誉教授。英詩研究会「デミタス」主宰（2000 年-）

主なる著書
　　『キーツ研究──自我の変容と理想主義』（北星堂）
　　『ジョン・キーツ──想像力の光と闇』（南雲堂）
　　『知の旅──髙橋雄四郎エッセイ集』（日本文学館）
　　『落穂を拾う』（音羽書房鶴見書店）
　　『キーツの想像力──妖精・牧歌』（音羽書房鶴見書店）

共訳
　　『ビート詩集』（国文社）

共著・他
　　Center and Circumference: Essays in English Romanticism.（邦題）
　　『中心と円周──イギリス・ロマン派学会創立 20 周年記念論文集』
　　（桐原書店）
　　『実践女子大学・公開市民講座シリーズ・第 1 集』（1986 年）（実践
　　女子大学・実践女子短期大学後援会編）
　　『髙橋雄四郎教授・J. V. ロプレスティ教授・退職記念集』（1998 年）
　　（実践英文科会）
　　『泉──次代への贈りもの・42 人の自分史観』（大分編）（星文社）
　　『戦争の記憶──問われているのは何か』（文京図書出版）

本籍地
　　大分市上戸次利光

遥かなる旅路
キーツ・エッセイ・漢詩

2017 年 9 月 9 日　初版発行

著　者　　高橋　雄四郎

発行者　　山口　隆史

印　刷　　株式会社太平印刷社

発行所　　株式会社 音羽書房鶴見書店

〒113–0033 東京都文京区本郷 4–1–14
TEL　03–3814–0491
FAX　03–3814–9250
URL: http://www.otowatsurumi.com
e-mail: info@otowatsurumi.com

Printed in Japan
ISBN978–4–7553–0402–6 C0095
組版編集　ほんのしろ／装幀　吉成美佐（オセロ）
製本　株式会社太平印刷社
©2017 by Yushiro Takahashi

資料図版

Apollon playing a Lite (Altes, Berlin)

筆者旅行行程図

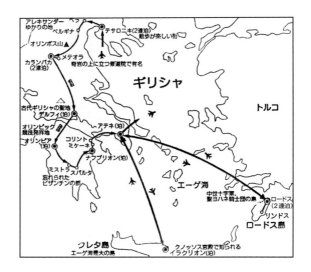

1 アレキサンダー大王の生誕地ベラより
  オリンポス山に向かう

2,3 オリンポスの山々

4 Artemis (Diana)

5 Apollon playing a Lite (Vatican)

6 Apollo 神殿跡

7 Apollo と Daphne
 (Roma, Borghese)

8 Apollo と Daphne (Louvre)

9 Satyre (Louvre)

10 Faun (Capitolino)

9, 10 は Bacchus とよく混同される。

11 Bacchus (Bode)

12 Eros (Louvre)

13 Psyche (Roma, Capitolino)

14 Love Triumphant
(Wallace Collection)

15 詩人の霊感 (Louvre)

17 Pandra
(Lady Lever Art Gallery)

16 Apollo et la Muse

18 Hope (Watts Gallery)

19 Fortuna (Capitolino)

20 Fortuna (Altes, Berlin)

21 La Tre Parche

22 Sleeping Endymion (Townly Room)

23 Sleeping Endymion
(N. Gallery, Berlin)

24 La Verite (D'Orsay)

25 Nike (Altes, Berlin)

26 Nike (N. Gallery)

27 楽園時代の私たちの祖先

28 Paradise Lost

29, 30　Arcadia（天上地、地上天）

故郷（アルカディア）は遠きにありて思うもの

p. 57–p. 58

31 私の故郷

32 先祖の墓

33 故郷の家

34 家に到る道

p. 58

35, 36 成大寺
(鶴ヶ城で討死したつわもの達の菩提寺)

p. 182

37, 38 鶴ヶ城跡

39 豊肥線

40 Sleeping Endymion
(Capitolino)

41 Hebe 青春の女神
(N. Gallery, Berlin)

p. 46

42 本間久雄先生

43 Keats House 元館長 Mrs Gee

44 筆者の自画像
Ode to a Nightingale ゆかりの場所

p. 48